A POPPY McVIE ADVENTURE

OPERATION *Bayou Justice*

Kimberli A. Bindschatel

Cover Design by Deranged Doctor Design

Published by Oliver-Heber Books

0 9 8 7 6 5 4 3 2 1

"Every kid got a turtle some time or other. Nobody can't keep a turtle though. They work at it and work at it, and at last one day they get out and away they go—off somewheres. It's like me."

~John Steinbeck, *The Grapes of Wrath*

Chapter One

I had a death grip on the edge of my seat as the airboat zipped along the surface of the water, mashing down swamp grass, skidding one way, then the other, its giant propeller roaring behind us. I swear he had the pedal all the way down, just for the hell of it.

Earl was in the driver's seat, the idiot Dalton and I had been assigned to babysit. Those weren't exactly the words our boss had used, but that's what we were doing just the same. Earl had managed to get himself arrested for possession and attempting to sell some protected turtles. Instead of fitting him with an ankle-bracelet, our boss got wind of the situation, rushed in to cut a plea deal with the guy, and put us undercover on twenty-four hour surveillance, hoping he'd lead us to his buyer—a man that, Earl had claimed, was a "big fish."

I wasn't sure Earl could find his way out of a paper bag. If he did, he'd slither out. With his greasy hair and muscled arms, he was exactly the kind of guy who made some women swoon—the ones who like those bad-boy types with the cocky swagger. Whatever the appeal, it eluded me. His "charm" made the hair on the back of my neck stand up. The way he looked at me made me feel like he was either undressing me with his eyes or secretly grinning, believing that he had somehow pulled the wool over my eyes. An annoying tee-hee-hee would erupt from his mouth at curious intervals that didn't seem to coincide with anything humorous. At least to my sense of humor.

Somehow, though, Dalton seemed to be able to ride on the same wavelength with him. Maybe it was a guy thing.

Special Agent Dalton and I had been partners now for several ops and he never ceased to amaze me at his ability to embody an undercover role and never flinch. Once we'd been assigned to this detail, he'd slipped right into playing the backwoods-turtle-poaching cousin of Earl without missing a beat. I swear, his knuckles were already bruised from dragging on the ground.

"Tee-hee-hee," he chuckled beside me as the airboat slowed.

"Hey, ya'll wanna drive?" Earl asked Dalton.

"Dude. Are you serious?" Dalton said, the perfect dopey-faced moron.

"Course not, man. Dis here boat is gov'ment property. I could lose my damn job." Earl wiped tobacco juice from the edge of his mouth with the back of his hand and grinned.

"Do they know you drive it like you stole it?" I said with a half-chuckle, pulling my hair back and retying it into a ponytail for the eighty-seventh time.

"Don you worry yer pretty little head there, 'possum cop'."

My teeth clamped together. "Stop calling me that. If you slip and say that when anyone else is around—"

"Awe, shush. You worry too damn much."

"I'm telling you right now—"

"I got it. I got it, girl. Ya don' hafta get so hot under da colla."

"And don't call her girl," Dalton said, I'm sure more for my benefit.

"Tee-hee-hee." He mashed down the throttle, throwing me back in the seat, and we were off again, speeding down the river of grass.

I glared at Dalton. *I swear I'm going to kill him.*

He shook his head. I wasn't sure, at that moment, whether I liked how Dalton could read my mind.

Earl's part-time job was to run the rural bookmobile, delivering books and other educational materials. His route went through some pretty remote areas in southern Louisiana. By remote, I mean, we were in the middle of a giant swamp on the edge of the Earth. These waterways were a labyrinth of tall grasses and patches of old cypress that all looked the same. I usually have an uncanny sense of direction, but I didn't want to admit that I had to rely solely on Earl's knowledge of the area to get us back out.

As we swung around the next bend, Earl throttled back to idle. The boat slowed in the water and just as we approached the shoreline, he whipped the bow around and eased the back edge of the boat up onto a mound of mushy dirt between a host of cypress knees. A clapboard shack with a rusted tin roof stood amid the trees, hiding from the midday sun. Out of the window came a shotgun barrel aimed directly at us.

"It's jus' me man! It's Earl!" Earl shouted. "We jus' here ta drop off da books ta ya. Dat's all."

"Why dat? You git it right dis time?" The gun jabbed in our direction. "Who dat wit ya?"

"Jus' my cousins visitin' from Ok-lee-homa. Taking 'em out on a scenic tour. Tee-hee-hee."

"Y'all jus' set it right der den," a gravely voice came back.

"Will do," Earl replied and dropped a tiny bundle of books on the ground. "See ya next week. Y'all take care now."

The barrel of the gun retreated back into the dark hole of a window. I couldn't help but wonder what kind of people could survive living out here like that, and what they'd be interested in reading. Whoever they were, they weren't going to let me get close enough to find out.

The huge blade whirred back to life and we were afloat again, zipping through the water once more.

Even in the breeze, the swamp felt like a sauna with the thermostat cranked up too high. My hair was beyond out of control. I was pretty sure we'd been put on this assignment as punishment. I'd pushed back hard on my last op, got myself entangled in some serious political crap, and Ms. Benetta Hyland, head of our team, wasn't too happy about it.

But she wasn't there, on the ground. It was easy to send orders from her office in Virginia, where things looked black and white. I was starting to realize that the Presidential Animal Task Force, of which I had proudly become a team member, wasn't about protecting animals at all. Sure, I understood that I was an agent of the government and my job was to enforce the law, but the law is mired in politics with a lot of gray areas. And no matter which way you sliced it, animals seem to always lose.

Like this very situation. Earl had been caught, red-handed, but he was offered a deal, and if he kept his end of the bargain, he'd get off, scot-free. Not even a slap on the wrist. Because. That's how it's done. To get the bigger fish.

Frankly, that whole concept was really starting to piss

me off. Sure, I get it. How else do we have a shot at stopping the trafficking? We have to get to the core of the problem. Take out the big hitters in the supply chain. But meanwhile, the day to day harm to animals continues. And jerks like this slaphappy jackass never spend a day in jail.

As far as I could tell, there was no evidence whatsoever that Earl had any serious relationship with an international exporter to hand over. Hyland, for whatever reason, seemed to think he did.

Dalton gave me that look. I swear he could read my mind.

Yeah, yeah, I know, I replied with my eyes.

Earl somehow managed to find the next "household" amid the dense foliage of the swamp. We got the same reception. Onward we went, making the weekly deliveries

Apparently, in these parts, no one has an official address, as they prefer to live off the grid, and any contact is made by slowly building trust. Two or three days a week, Earl sets out on the airboat to hand-deliver books and other supplies, some vital, such as prescriptions. So, here we were.

Earl maneuvered the boat in a ninety-degree turn, then back to the right in another ninety-degree turn, and suddenly we were among some old-growth cypress trees, as tall as any I'd ever seen. Spanish moss dripped from the limbs, and the sunlight streamed through into the dark, giving the swamp an eerie feeling.

He slowed as the waves from the boat lapped off the trunks, swirling around the knees of the trees, and brought the boat nearly to a stop. His eyes were darting around looking through the brush on the edge of the water.

"What are you looking for?" I asked.

"I ain't lookin' fa nuttin'."

He was looking for something. I scanned the water

trying to see what it might be. Then something caught my eye. A line had been tied to a tree limb and pulled taut into the water.

"What is it?" I asked.

"It ain't nuttin' y'all got ta worry 'bout," he said.

He pushed down on the throttle, and I spun on him, making him stop. "I want to see what that is."

"It ain't nuttin'. jus' an ole anchor somebody done dropped in da water."

"Let it go," Dalton said, crossing his arms.

"You know I can't."

"Oh, I know."

"Earl, pull up right beside it."

He huffed, but did as I told him.

As we got closer, the line zigzagged around in the water.

"Something's caught on that," I said.

"It's a gator bait line," Dalton said.

"It's not alligator hunting season right now," I said to Earl, making it clear that I knew that.

"Exactly," said Earl. "Dat's why we outta not touch nuttin' and best be mindin' our own business."

"Seems like it was your business," I said. "I saw you looking. You knew that was there. Have you been hunting gators off-season? Because you know that would nullify your plea bargain."

"Damn, woman, yer like a dog wit a bone. I ain't done nuttin' wrong. A man can look around. Who knows who put up dat bait? Could be anyone."

"Well, I know you know how to take care of it. Just get that gator off that line now."

"What? Now why in da hell would I do dat?"

I stood up, hands on my hips. "Because I said so."

He huffed, annoyed with me, but did I care? Nope.

With the deft hands of an experienced gator hunter, Earl took a hold of that line, hauled it in hand over hand, and within seconds he had a four-foot gator up and over the edge of the boat and flopping around on the floor.

The poor thing was in a panic. Its jaws were snapping and the tail was whipping side to side as it bounced to and fro in the bottom of the aluminum boat. Earl was chuckling, his stupid tee hee hee, tee hee hee. He slammed his foot down on the back of its neck and it froze in place.

"Well, now what da ya want me ta do?"

"Put it back in the water," I said. "What else?"

He shook his head and gritted his yellow teeth. "Whateva you say, ma'am."

"And don't call me ma'am."

He grabbed a hold of the snout of that gator with one hand and yanked the hook out with the other, then took a hold of its tail, lifted it up, and tossed it high into the air. It flailed around, airborne, freaking out in the momentary weightlessness, before falling into the water with a big splash.

I shook my head and rolled my eyes. *Jackass.*

"Now what?"

I plopped back down in the seat. "Now get going. Let's finish this route so we can get out of this damn sauna."

"I don't suppose you know who put that line out?" asked Dalton.

"Nope. Shore don't. But what's it matter? Even if I done it, I don' have ta tell y'all. I got me a get-outta-jail-free card." With another tee hee hee, he stomped on the gas and we were off again.

I clenched my fists tight and then released them again. "That's not how it works," I shouted over the engine, realizing as I did that he had no clue either way, and it didn't matter anyhow. Hyland would probably pardon him for shooting the governor if it got her what she wanted.

My boss was determined that this guy could lead us somewhere, yet, after a month in the swamp, we had zero information. If you asked me, it was a complete waste of time. But here I was, nonetheless.

Dalton and I had our job cut out for us. I had no idea how we were going to get this guy to do what we needed. From the moment we'd arrived, he'd been giving us the royal runaround. Wouldn't answer any questions. He just kept saying, "He'll be in touch. He'll be in touch."

I was convinced he had no connection at all, and he was just dragging us along for the ride. He seemed to get a glorious kick out of the whole situation and had been enjoying getting under my skin.

When I'd dreamed of being a wildlife agent, living in a floating shack in the middle of the bayou with this idiot for days on end wasn't part of the vision.

And to add to my concerns, Dalton wasn't acting like himself either. While I'd been digging myself neck-deep into wolf politics in Idaho on my last op, he'd gone off to Africa to investigate my father's murder—without telling me. Now he was tight-lipped and even more evasive when I tried to ask him about it. When he first got back, I was so relieved, I didn't think to question too much. But now… something wasn't right.

Then there was the heat. Who could live in this oven? It wasn't helping matters.

Finally, with my hair in a tangled mess, and my tank top soaked in sweat, we arrived back at Earl's palace, a floating fish camp tucked among the trees, half covered in moss. The place was long and narrow, like a floating wood-sided mobile home, with a covered porch on one end and a tiny bedroom on the other with a smaller porch where an open-air bathroom had been fashioned with a Porta Potty and a sun shower. The rest of the interior was one open room with a smelly couch, a card table with four plastic chairs, and a kitchenette which included a hot plate and a full-sized refrigerator full of beer. An old air conditioner unit hung in the window, but the damn thing didn't work. At least that's what Earl said. I suspect he didn't want to pay for the gasoline to run the generator any more than he had to.

He pulled up alongside the over-sized raft, tied off the lines, then killed the engine.

"I need a shower," I said.

"By all means," Earl said, gesturing toward the backside of the houseboat.

I didn't have a problem with that kind of a shower; I'd lived in the woods, been a camper, living out of a backpack my whole life. But there was something about Earl's attitude that irritated me, like he had one over on us, that this was all a game to him. *I know, I know.* I needed to adjust my own attitude. It was all part of the job. But that didn't mean I didn't want to drop kick him into the muck.

With my towel in hand, I headed to the back side of the raft, peeled off my sweaty clothes, and let the water soak in my hair and flow down my back.

"It's only temporary," I said aloud. "This too shall pass." Soon, Earl will lead us to the exporter, and then we'll be trailing *him.* Earl will be behind us. *A distant memory.*

Chapter Two

Out on the porch, I plopped down in a plastic lawn chair in the shade next to Dalton with a comb in my hand and tried to work at the tangles in my crazy hair. Dalton and Earl had already cracked open a couple of beers.

Earl slithered onto the porch, gave the swamp a quick scan, then turned and leaned back on the railing.

The old rotten wood creaked, and I wished it would give way.

"You don' like it here much, do ya?" he said.

"Kinda hoped I'd never have to set foot in Louisiana, actually," I said, a little too sardonically.

Dalton turned to stare at me. "Really? Why?"

I stopped combing my hair for a moment. *Why did I open my big mouth?* I started combing again, hoping Dalton wouldn't pursue it. "Nothing. Really."

"Oh, come on," Dalton said. "I figured you'd love the wilderness here."

I stared at the water, where dragonflies swooped down on the mosquitoes hovering just above the surface.

Suddenly the reason felt ridiculous. I looked him right in the eye. "Um, nope."

He gave me that look. "What gives?"

"I just have a weird fear, is all. It's irrational. But, you know, we all have those little quirks."

A grin crept across his face. "Quirks? Oh, you've got quirks."

"I'm human," I said, trying to sound all flirty, hoping he'd let it go.

"So?"

"Yeah, what gives wit dat?" said Earl, wiping his nose with the back of his hand. "You too good for us or somethin'?"

Ugh. "Okay, fine. When I was a young kid, like, I don't know, ten, I accidentally saw a scene from the movie *Angel Heart* and I've harbored an irrational fear of the Louisiana bayou ever since. End of story."

"What scene?" Dalton asked.

"Huh?"

"What scene? From the movie?"

How do I back out of this? "Um, it was, you know, where the heart got ripped out."

His eyebrows shot up. "You just happened to see that one—"

"And the chicken beheading. And the boiling pot of murder scene." I huffed. *Geez.* "Okay, so, I watched the whole movie."

Dalton sat back. "Wow, that's dark. Definitely not a film for a ten year old."

"Yeah, no kidding. It's a whole voodoo thing where the devil owns your soul. It's creepy, you know."

Earl let rip a rolling laughter that ended in his obnoxious tee-hee-hee, snuffling.

Jerk. "You know what, I'm going to call in," I said, pushing up from the chair.

"I gotta take a piss," Earl said with a burp. He jostled around toward the water, unzipping his pants.

"Dude, bathroom," Dalton said, gesturing in that direction.

"Whatever," he grumbled and pushed by me.

After a moment, Dalton said, "Don't let him get under your skin."

"I'm just going to go make that call," I said. "We haven't talked to Hyland in a while."

"Fine," Dalton said softly, his eyes showing his concern. "But it's not like anything is happening around here." His gaze swung in the direction Earl had gone. "We're here for the duration. Settle in. Have a beer."

"I know, but I got a question for her." It wasn't true, but I'd had enough of being cooped up here in the fish camp; I needed some space.

I got into the little rowboat and rowed about a quarter of a mile away, just far enough where I couldn't be heard, and took three deep breaths before I dialed in.

To my surprise, she answered on the first ring. "Any news?"

"No. Nothing. Just checking in. But I did want to talk to you. I'm wondering if this is really the best use of our time. Now that I've spent considerable time with him, I don't think Earl's the right partner here. He just doesn't seem, I don't know, you know."

I could feel her annoyance through the phone. "No, I don't know. And it sounds like you don't either. Hence your assignment: get information."

I drew in a breath, steadying myself to speak calmly. "I guess what I'm saying is that, yes, this guy got caught in a buy—and deserves to be behind bars by the way—but I don't think the plea-bargain means anything to him. I feel like he's just stringing us along for fun."

"You *feel* this?"

"Well, yeah. My gut's telling me—"

"So you have no evidence?"

"Well, nothing concrete. I'm just saying it doesn't feel right. He's not forthcoming. It's like this is all a game to him."

There was a pause. "His attitude is irrelevant."

"Irrelevant? He's supposed to help lead us to the exporter and I don't think he cares if he ever does. It's like he's enjoying having us here so he can—"

"Well, I will take that under consideration."

"I'm saying he's rotten. To the core. There's no way this is going to work. In fact, I think he might—"

"You seem to be under the impression that your opinion matters here. You've got your assignment."

I sucked in a mouthful of air. "Wait. Are you saying that you don't care that he's a waste of time or you don't care that that's what I think?"

"McVie, do your job."

The line went dead. I stared at my phone. *Dammit!*

I looked around at the water, the trees, the scorching sun, taking it all in at once. *What am I doing here?* Was this really what I'd signed up for? Somehow, being on the Presidential animal task force had seemed like the ultimate position, a place to finally make a difference. I was supposed to stop the worst of the worst, put big bad guys away, rid the world of those who'd harm animals.

And I was stuck in a swamp with Earl, a two-bit jerk-off who thought this whole thing was a joke and a boss who didn't care what I thought at all.

Somewhere, something had gone wrong. This wasn't

where I was supposed to be. Maybe my mother had been right.

No! Stop it.

But looking for a different job, a different role wouldn't be so bad. Maybe I just needed a little sign. Something to let me know this whole career hadn't become a complete waste of time.

My phone rang in my hand. It was my friend Chris. *Okay, weird.* He always knew what I was thinking before I was thinking it, and had an insane, crazy ability to help me sort things out and see clearly.

Relief flushed over me. He would help me sort this out. I clicked to receive the call.

"Hey, were you reading my mind all the way from… where are you now?" He's a flight attendant with Delta Airlines, so I never knew where he was or what time zone he was in. He could've been anywhere in the world.

"Beijing. Where are you?"

"I'm sitting in a rowboat in the middle of a Louisiana bayou."

"Oh, well that's nice," he said, his tone flat. He didn't seem surprised at all.

"Wait, it must be the middle of the night there. And what do you mean, that's nice? I'm on constant lookout for water moccasins. I'm surviving on canned beans. And it's so hot and muggy it's like breathing soup out here. There's nothing nice about it."

"Uh-huh."

Usually that kind of description would illicit a sarcastic retort. "Chris, what's going on?

"Nothing. I'm just bored."

"You don't sound bored. You sound upset. What's going on?"

Silence.

"Come on now, you know I can tell something's wrong."

"No, that's not how this works. I usually call you, and our phone conversations are always about you, and what's going on with you, so I'm asking what's going on with you."

"See, that's a red flag right there. Usually you complain about that, so, ha, you think I don't pay attention. Cough it up. What's going on?"

He sighed. "I don't know. I'm just feeling restless, I guess. Truly, I want to hear about you."

"No you don't."

"Okay, I don't. But tell me anyway."

"Okay, I will. But you tell me first. I can tell something's wrong."

"Not wrong. Just… Fine. Life is just, I don't know, not that exciting anymore."

That didn't sound like Chris at all. He was usually so upbeat the chandeliers would shake. "Well, how's the dating going?"

"Don't even start with me."

"You're just feeling a little depressed because of everything that's happened. Ooooooh!" I squealed with delight. This was it. "Why don't you fly down here to New Orleans? I'll take a couple of days off. Dalton can handle this babysitting job. It's not like anything is happening. Besides, I think he's actually enjoying it. Aren't you always telling me I should take some time off? Let's do it. We'll get some of that bad coffee and those beignet donut things with extra powdered sugar and wander around looking for trouble. We could go shopping."

"You hate shopping."

"I know. See, that's how much I miss you. I'd go shopping with you. Say you'll come."

There was a long pause before Chris answered. "I'm not sure that's a good idea. Whenever you want me to come around, I end up dressed up in some crazy getup and playing the bad guy, and getting shot at or something. I don't think I can handle another adventure like Costa Rica."

I sighed. I knew what this was about. "Is that because it makes you think of Doug?"

More silence.

Chris had met Doug while visiting me in Costa Rica. They got engaged, then Doug was killed by a Mexican cartel.

"This will be different. I promise," I said.

"Of course it will." He sighed. "Those carefree days are gone."

"C'mon, now. You're just in a funk right now."

"I know. I can't help but think, what if we could go back in time? What if I hadn't met Doug? What if you hadn't hooked up with Noah? What if…"

"Don't do this to yourself, Chris."

"What if you would've hit it off with that hot Australian at the pool? What was his name?"

"Kevin?"

"Yeah, Kevin. And you know how you can get, like a dog with a bone. If you would've followed him to the end of the earth to crack your case, instead of Noah, then I never would have met Doug and…"

"Okay, it's official. I'm taking time off and you're flying here to spend some time with me."

"Nah."

"Chris!"

"I'm fine. Besides, you've got work to do. It sounds fun to you right now, but as soon as I got there, you'd be all involved in your job and wouldn't actually be able to break free. So, let's just do this thing we do, you tell me about what's going on in your life, I help, and we both feel better."

This didn't sound like my friend Chris. Something was wrong, very wrong, but I wasn't sure what else to do from a rowboat in the middle of a swamp. "Okay, fine. Here's what's going on. I'm stuck hanging out with this backwoods jerk who likes to sell animals for profit, you know the usual, except this guy's a little more, er, eccentric. In a whole month here, we've gotten absolutely nowhere. No clues. No new intel. Nothing. Nada. And I'm about to lose it. And to add to that, my boss thinks I'm an emotional little girl who can't focus. Or something. Maybe I am. Come to think of it, maybe it's just the heat. It's so freaking hot here, and you know how I handle heat."

"I know it does wonders for your hair."

"No kidding. I look like I stuck my finger in an electrical socket." I got a small giggle for that one. "Seriously, Chris. I'm worried about you."

"Don't worry, Poppy girl. I'm just feeling a little down. It's no big deal. I feel better already just hearing your voice. You're right, maybe I'll catch a flight to New Orleans."

I grinned. "Now you're talking. "

"I'll let you know when I can swing it. Meanwhile, get yourself a glass of iced tea, stick your feet in some cool water, and remember you're saving the world."

Eye roll. "If only."

"Every little bit counts. Now get yourself some tea."

"I'll do that." I hung up feeling uneasy. Something was off. More than off. Something was very wrong. I'd call and check on him a little later. He'd be fine, though, I told myself. If Chris was anything, he was resilient. He'd always been my rock.

He'd be fine.

I hoped.

I took hold of the oar handles, dug them into the murky water, and rowed back to the fish camp.

Iced tea was a good idea. I poured a glass, dragged the lawn chair to the shady side of the porch, and plopped down and closed my eyes. This would all be over soon.

"Hey, my buddy jus' called, and they's all going on over to da bar pit for some target practice."

I opened my eyes to see Earl standing in front of me with a shot gun in his hand. I leapt up from the chair. "You can't handle a firearm while you're on probation. It's violating the plea agreement."

"Well, I jus' don' know how I can keep dat agreement and, *quote*,"—he made quote marks in the air with his grubby fingers—"act like my normal self and go about my normal everyday activities, *quote*, if I don' go shootin' some damn beer cans down at da bar pit wit my buddies." He cocked his head toward Dalton and fixed his beady eyes on him. "Ain't dat da truth?"

Dalton shrugged. "He's got a point."

Oh my God, seriously? I drew in a long breath. "Sure, Earl, let's go shoot some beer cans."

He handed me a four-ten shotgun and had another twelve-gauge for Dalton to use. Who knew he had so many firearms here in the fish camp? Had they been in the rafters?

We got into his fishing boat and sped off toward shore, where we were met by his buddy in a pickup truck. Of course he had three other buddies with him, so we had to pile into the bed of the truck to ride over to the bar pit, whatever that was anyway.

By way of introduction Earl grunted something like,

"Dese here are my cousins visitin' from Oklahoma." Nobody seemed to care. Simple as that, they nodded and accepted our presence just on Earl's say-so.

The bar pit turned out to be a muddy pond with aluminum cans scattered about that had been shredded by gunfire and left to rot in the heat.

Al, one of Earl's buddies, the driver of the pickup truck, dragged a plastic garbage bag full of cans to a log that had somehow survived the onslaught of bullets. He set up a row of cans, one at a time with one hand, in slow-motion it seemed, as he, of course, had a full can of beer in the other hand.

"Ladies first," he said and nodded at me with a snicker. I assumed the women in these parts could handle a firearm, but then one never knew. His attitude seemed to be a bit condescending. I caught the expression on Dalton's face. Was he smirking?

I loaded the four-ten with four shells, brought the butt of the gun to my shoulder, and raised it to take aim. With my finger on the trigger, I let loose. Fire, pump, fire, pump, fire, pump, fire, pump. The empty shells ejected out the side—1, 2, 3, 4—as the beer cans magnificently blasted to pieces.

Earl's google eyes just about bugged out of his head. I don't know why he was the one so surprised. He knew I was a federal agent. *Idiot.*

Al whooped it up. "Wow, girl, where'd you learna shoot like dat?"

"I don't know what you mean," I said. *And don't call me girl.* "I grew up in Oklahoma. It's what we do."

I wasn't sure why, but the guys lost interest in shooting beer cans all of a sudden.

Al gestured for us to get back in the pickup truck. "I jus' wanna check somethin' out down the road."

There were shrugs all around. They didn't care, it was something to do.

So, back into the pickup truck we went. We bumped along down the dusty road, then Al suddenly slammed on the brakes. I tumbled into Dalton.

"Well look-y dere," Al said, his hand stretched out from the driver side window. The transmission was shifted into park as he climbed out of the truck.

Alongside the dirt road, abandoned in the woods, was an old sofa, all weathered and torn. It was wood-framed with brown plaid cushions made circa 1964.

Before I knew it, Al had a tow strap wrapped around that old couch and attached to the bumper.

The other two buddies fell out of the passenger side of the truck and plopped down on the couch. One of them, Ernie or Jimmy, I don't know which, said, "Let's do dis thang."

What thing?

Al was back in the driver seat and shifting into drive before I got my mouth clamped shut. I turned to Dalton. "You have got to be kidding."

He winked at me. "What? You've never been couch surfing before?"

With Ernie on one side and Jimmy on the other, each with one hand clamped onto an armrest and the other holding a can of beer, Al stomped on the gas pedal and we were off. As the tow strap became taut, the couch tipped back and they let out loud whoops. Those boys' legs flopped around with every bump as they hooted and hollered and giggled like children.

Al took a corner and the couch skidded off to the left, off the road into the bushes, ripping off leaves and branches. The boys just leaned into it and laughed louder.

After about five minutes of the shenanigans, Al

brought the truck to a stop, leaned out the window and said, "Who's up next?"

Dalton got up and hopped off the tailgate. "Hell yeah, and I won't be sitting on my ass like you pansies. That's not how you ride a couch."

One stride and he was standing on top of the couch, one foot on the cushion, his other foot on the back. He had it tipped up a little bit, perfectly balanced.

I shook my head. What the hell was he thinking? I climbed up onto the couch next to him. He looked at me and I looked at him. He shrugged and muttered, "Might as well have a little fun while we're here."

Dalton let out a whoop and hollered, "Make it happen, Captain."

Al spun the tires and I about flipped off the back of that couch into the air, but Dalton grabbed me by the arm, and we skidded and bounced down the dirt road.

It reminded me of Noah, a guy I'd met in Costa Rica on my first official op. He'd surfed on the top of the van of a wildlife trafficker, all the way down a mountain and into town where we nailed the guy for stuffing snakes full of drugs.

This was one crazy profession.

Chris was right about one thing. When it came to Noah, I had been like a dog with a bone. That was my first op and I had something to prove. Since then, I'd learned so much. Mostly from Dalton, though I hated to admit it. He'd been a steady, solid influence and working with him had helped me understand some patience, diplomacy, even compliance. When we weren't bickering.

I squeezed his hand. He was right. This couch surfing was kind of fun. It was kind of like bull riding, see who can last longer than eight seconds.

An hour later, after we switched on and off several

times with the other boys, and were thoroughly covered in dust, we were declared the winners.

"I need ta take a dump," Earl declared. He eyed Al. "At yer place."

"Why my place?" Al said, his lip curled up in disgust.

"Cuz I said so."

Earl stared and for some reason Al gave in. He put the truck in gear and we bounced back down the road.

Al's place was at the end of a long two-track, past a cable gate. He pulled up to the dilapidated porch of a log cabin and killed the engine.

"I might be a while," Earl said then disappeared inside.

Dalton and I exchanged a what-the-hell glance.

Ernie and Jimmy mumbled something about more beer and went toward an outbuilding, presumably one that held an old refrigerator full.

Dalton was already doing his scanning-for-threats thing.

My eyes landed on the pond and I caught sight of a ripple. A turtle surfaced, for a brief moment. A huge turtle. I jumped out of the back of the truck and headed for the pond. Al followed right behind me.

"Is that an alligator snapping turtle?" I asked.

"Shore is," he said with a grin. "A biggin'."

I opened my eyes wide. "Yeah? How big?"

"Biggest one around." I swear his chest puffed out a little.

Alligator snapping turtles, especially one that size are very rare. They've been trapped nearly to extinction and are a protected species in most of the United States. Unfortunately, not here in Louisiana. In fact, the current trap limit is one per person, per day. Considering they are long-lived, with a low reproduction rate, the law is outrageous. Any local will say they can't be found anywhere anymore anyway. Once turtle soup became part of gourmet cuisine culture, the commercial trappers arrived, and that was the end of them.

So how was it that Al had one? Another ripple appeared. *Make that two.*

I turned to face him. "I bet you don't want nobody to know."

"Ain't nobody round here stupid enough to come on my land and steal my turtles."

"You been raising 'em since they was young, then?" I asked, keeping my eyes locked with his.

He fidgeted a moment. "Yep. My whole life." His gaze broke free and back toward the cabin. "What's keeping Earl anyways?"

A few years ago, a woman and her two sons from Louisiana got busted for possession of alligator snappers they'd poached over the state line in Texas, where they are protected, and brought back home to their private pond, just like this one. These turtles, at maximum weight, can be sold for well over a thousand dollars each. This pond was a little gold mine for Al. He'd probably been doing the same thing to acquire them.

But these weren't the same turtles being exported by whomever Hyland was after. Right now, there was nothing I could do about it. I made a note to self to see if Al was on anyone's radar.

"Seems like you got something nobody else has," I said.

With a bang of a door slamming behind him, Earl sauntered out onto the porch. He looked right at me and that shit-eating grin spread across his face. "Them's some nice looking' turtles, eh?"

I nodded.

"Better eatin' den a hip-po-pot-o-moose."

I glanced back at Al.

Al shook his head. "Gov'ment shit."

"What are you talking about?"

"Nothing." He turned back toward Earl and hollered, "Can we can get goin' now or what?"

Earl shrugged and headed for the truck.

When we finally got back to the fish camp, Earl seemed tired, like it actually had been a long day, and he wasn't happy to see his girlfriend Sandy sitting on the porch. Wild-eyed, hands gesturing in every direction, she lit into him before we even had the lines tied.

"Where da hell you been, Earl? Me and Piddles been waitin' here for, like, well all damn day."

"I been out."

A chihuahua yipped and spun. Piddles, I assumed.

Earl headed for the bedroom and Sandy followed him in, slamming the door behind her. Not that it mattered, we could hear every word.

Dalton stretched out on the couch, leaned his head back and closed his eyes, seemingly oblivious. I slumped down onto my cot. *Maybe my mom was right. Maybe I should have worked at a non-profit, spending my days lobbying for reform somewhere in some cushy, air-conditioned office.*

Before I could get to another thought, Earl and Sandy had made up, apparently, because the sounds coming from his room were most distinctly the sounds of two people getting along quite well.

Piddles jumped onto the cot with me and snuggled under my arm.

Ugh. My country for a pair of ear plugs.

Chapter Three

I woke to the sweet aroma of coffee percolating on the stove. I rolled off my cot, springing little Piddles into the air. I'd forgotten about him. "Sorry little buddy," I whispered. He shook it off. I sauntered over to see Dalton already had two ceramic mugs in hand and was smiling at me.

He leaned toward me and whispered in my ear, "You're so beautiful in the morning."

I rolled my eyes. "Thanks, but you can't be serious." My hair looked like a family of pigeons had taken up residence.

"Are you kidding?" His hand slid from my hip to the small of my back. "I'm going crazy without you."

I looked up at him. "I'm right here."

A little moan rumbled in his throat. "Yeah, but not close enough."

I gave him a quick kiss. "That will have to do for now."

Those eyes of his seemed to melt. "You're killing me."

"What do they say? Absence makes the heart grow fonder," I said with a grin.

"Yeah, absence. Not abstinence."

He poured the dark brown nectar-of-the-gods into a mug for me and we went out onto the porch and sat down to enjoy the peaceful morning. Birds chittered away as they flitted through the Spanish moss-draped branches above. Frogs croaked in the weeds, and a gentle breeze whispered through the tree tops, though the heat was already pressing in.

Dalton leaned toward me. "I'm a little worried that we won't be able to keep Earl out of trouble, and we'll lose this chance. What do you think?"

I nodded. "He's a wildcard. I don't like it. Not to mention, he's an utter ass. I bet Tom and Mike have it easy with Johnny boy."

Tom and Mike were our partners on the team. When Earl had been arrested, he was with another suspect, John Sebastian. Tom and Mike had been assigned to babysit John, while we got stuck with Earl.

"I wonder if Johnny has a girlfriend." I rolled my eyes. "The walls in this fish camp are a little thin."

Dalton's eyebrows went up. "I don't know what you're talking about."

I slapped him on the arm.

He leaned in closer and whispered, "Seriously, why do you hate this guy so much? He's just like every other perp we've had to deal with."

"Yeah, and I've hated every other perp we've had to deal with. You know that."

"Do we have to have the conversation all over again?"

I had to take a deep breath before responding. Dalton was right. We'd been over it before. Our job was to get the biggest fish, to always keep our eye on the big picture. We used the Earls of the world to get what we needed to move up the chain. Sometimes it got us nowhere. But it ground my ass to let him off. This guy wouldn't be reformed, wouldn't change his stripes. He didn't care one bit about the animals, never would. All he saw were dollar signs. He'd be back at it the moment we left. "No. I'm just saying. The man has no remorse. He has no respect for the plea agreement. He thinks he's got a get-out-of-jail-free card. And he kinda does. I can't stand it. You know me." I leaned toward him and whispered, "What really gets my goat is that I know damn well he has jack-shit to hand over. Hyland has lost her mind on this one. This is a waste of time and you know it."

"Maybe, maybe not."

I turned to stare at him. "How do you do it? Knowing the odds? Maybe we're just wasting our time? Not making a difference at all?"

He shrugged.

"I'm trying, you know," I said. *Trying not to wring his neck.*

"Good," Dalton said with an affirmative nod. "New subject then?"

I grinned. "Good idea. Tell me about Africa."

I took a sip of my coffee as I watched Dalton tense. His eyes locked onto something in the distance.

"I don't understand why you went, without telling me, and why you won't talk about it now."

"There's nothing more to talk about. I told you everything I know."

I leaned closer and whispered, "Bullshit. You've said vague stuff about vague things and it's all been so... vague."

He crossed his arms and wouldn't look me in the eye.

"You were there for two weeks. You found out *something*."

He turned to face me. "I did. And I told you. Your dad was trying to get information about the poachers for a local group. You said it yourself, he wasn't trained for that. He poked around too much, got caught, and paid the price."

"But that doesn't make any sense."

"No, you just don't want it to."

Anger flamed up inside me and my damn cheeks caught fire.

His expression softened. "It's not a stretch to think he'd keep that from you. You were a child. You were twelve years old."

"Yeah, but…"

"Yeah, but nothing. You need to let it go."

My muscles tensed. *Let it go?* What did he know about having a parent murdered? "Don't you dare tell me what to feel."

He frowned. "That's not what I meant."

"I know there's something you're not telling me."

He shook his head and lifted his coffee cup to his lips.

"I'm not a child now, you know."

His head snapped my way. "What?"

"A child. Though you insist on treating me like one."

"That's not fair."

"Isn't it? You're holding something back, like I can't be trusted with information. And you're telling yourself it's to protect me, to keep me safe, to keep me from running off and doing something rash."

The muscle in his jaw tightened. "Yeah? Maybe I am."

I sat up straight in the chair. "So you don't deny it? I thought we were past this in our relationship." I let out a little involuntary huff. "You don't trust me."

"You aren't exactly known for being level-headed."

I stared. I had no words. No response. He was admitting it. The condescending ass.

I drew in a deep breath and turned away.

We sat in silence until our coffee was gone, him stone-faced, me stewing. I got up to refill my cup.

Leaning on the tiny counter, I stared into the black liquid. What was I doing? I was a grown-ass woman and I kept getting told, over and over again, that I was too this, too that. Too emotional. Too reactive. Too mouthy. Too opinionated. Well, I'd had enough. What I'd been is too tolerant. If Dalton wouldn't be truthful with me, then what kind of relationship were we in? Certainly not the kind I wanted to have. Yeah. No. Yep. I needed to get out of here.

I glanced at him, relaxing in the chair on the porch. *Just focus on the operation for now. Deal with Dalton later.*

Deep breath.

When I sat back down, I gestured toward Earl's room. "I wonder what kind of day we're going to have with him today, what kind of crap he's going to pull. I swear he's doing all this on purpose just to test us."

"What if he is? He can throw whatever he wants at me," Dalton said. "I'm getting paid to be here and he can't hold out forever." He reached over and took my hand in his. "Look at it this way, we get to spend time together, and we're not getting shot at."

"Sounds boring," I said and pulled my hand away.

Earl's book route took us through another rural area, but this time in his pickup truck. The day couldn't have been any more boring as I sat in the back, my hair whipping around into a tangled mess as he left book after book on front porches.

My anger toward Dalton grew. He may have had more experience, or maybe a more even temperament, but that didn't give him the right to decide what I could or couldn't handle. He'd say it was out of love, but I call bullshit. It wasn't a good way to start a relationship, and I wasn't having any of it.

Whatever he had learned in Africa, I could find out on my own. And that's exactly what I was going to do. I didn't need Dalton to tell me anything. Whatever happened to my dad, I could handle it. I didn't need his help either. Especially if his help meant keeping me in the dark.

At the end of the work day, Earl declared it was Thursday, and on Thursdays, he always goes down to the Rock 'n' Rollin' Bowling Alley, where he and Sandy dance to the zydeco band.

"Don't worry. You don't hafta keep up," he said.

I looked at Dalton and rolled my eyes. *See what I mean? Cocky son of a bitch.*

The Rock 'n' Rollin' Bowling Alley was about a twenty-minute drive from the fish camp. We picked up Sandy on the way and the four of us crammed into the cab of the truck, arms touching, all sticky while Earl blasted the radio.

When we arrived, Earl couldn't find a parking spot, so he left the truck in the ditch along the side of the road, not the slightest thought about the legality of it.

Apparently this was the happening place on a Thursday night. There was a line at the door to get in.

I like to dance and I was pleasantly surprised to find out on our first op together that Dalton was quite the dancer. I'd never danced to zydeco music, but I was confident we *could* keep up.

Once inside, I was surprised at the size of the place. Twelve bowling lanes, a restaurant area, and a large dance floor, at the head of which was a stage with a ten-piece band. Pink and blue neon lights pulsed around the stage throwing beams of color onto the dancers as they spun and twirled. The place lived up to its name. It was a' rockin'.

To my surprise, though, it was a family affair. People of

all ages—moms, dads, aunts, uncles, all the kids—danced together, taking turns spinning around the wood floor. The lead singer belted out tunes as he strummed a washboard mounted to his belly while his bandmate pumped an accordion. The beat was contagious—fast paced and upbeat. I'd never heard anything like it, and I loved it.

It seemed everybody in the place knew Earl. Sandy followed him around in his shadow as he worked the room, all jovial, never acknowledging her presence. What she saw in him, I'll never know, but she seemed devoted.

Soon, they took to the dance floor and zipped around, darting between other dancers, for three or four tunes before they finally took a break to get a beer. But the break didn't last long, and they were back out there.

Dalton and I managed to keep up. I admitted, the couch surfing had been kind of fun, in its crazy-ass-backwoods kind of way. But here, I truly was having a good time as Dalton spun me round and round. He was a great dancer. And a good person, I just... Why couldn't he treat me as an equal?

There were a lot of people here and I had a weird feeling about this setting. I kept my eye on Earl. Something wasn't right. Maybe it was the way he'd explained his buy-sell arrangement during the plea hearing. It was vague, with little substance. Hyland was convinced he was the key to finding the exporter, but I wasn't. His testimony had sounded like a lot of hot air to me. But there was something about the way he was acting tonight...

"I don't understand you," Dalton said.

My neck snapped back. "What?"

"Aren't you enjoying this?"

"The dancing?" What was he talking about?

"The dancing, being undercover, on the cusp of catching a bad guy. Isn't that what you love? I mean, isn't that why we got on this team? I thought it was what you wanted."

"Where is this coming from all of a sudden?"

"I just don't understand you. Here we are, on this big case, deep undercover, out for a night on the town, dancing together and you're still so unhappy."

I came to a halt on the dance floor. "Seriously? You think I wanted the *lifestyle*?"

"I don't know what you want." He frowned. "And I don't think you know either."

My teeth clenched together. "You can be such a jerk, you know that?"

"I'm just saying."

I spun away from him. *Just focus on the job.*

I glanced around the bowling alley, looking for Earl. The last thing I needed was to be distracted by my issues with Dalton.

Sandy was standing alone by an empty table. *Crap.* Where had Earl gone?

"We've lost Earl," I said. Dalton's eyes immediately started scanning the room, the Navy SEAL training kicking in.

I went right to Sandy. "Where'd Earl go?"

She shrugged sheepishly. "He said he had to take a piss, but…"

"But what?"

"It's been a while."

Dalton bee-lined for the men's room. He was back out in two seconds, shaking his head. Earl wasn't in there. I went one way and he went the other.

It didn't take long, and I found Earl. He'd gone out the back door, just outside the glow of a streetlight, and had another woman bent over the trunk of a car. They were going at it like a couple of cats in heat. What a dirtbag.

A stroke of inspiration. I could use this to my advantage. I marched back into the building, took Sandy by the arm, and told her to follow me. We weren't two steps out the back door when her eyes landed on Earl and the other woman, and she shrieked like a barn cat. She flung expletives so fast, it sounded like one long word.

Earl pulled away and slowly zipped his zipper and tightened his belt. "Back off, woman. You don't own me."

Sandy burst into tears and stomped off toward the ladies room. I followed. I admit, I was really feeling for Sandy. I didn't have to do that. But maybe it was for the best. And this was my chance to get some information from her.

Dalton seemed to know what I was up to, so he stayed with Earl.

Sandy soaked a handful of paper towels in the sink and blotted her face, wiping mascara from under her eyes. "I jus' don't understand. I thought he loved me."

I nodded.

"I thought we was gonna get married. How can he do this to me?"

"I'm sorry, Sandy. I don't know what to say. Earl seems like"—I felt like I had sand on my tongue as I pushed the words from my mouth—"a nice guy."

"Nice guy? Well he… I don't know. Sometimes he ain't so nice." There was a pause. "The bastard."

Like when he's screwing some other woman in the parking lot? "What do you mean?" I had no idea if this was going anywhere, but building a rapport with her would be helpful.

"I swear, sometimes I think he just with me 'cause of ma job. Most time, he'd rather be with the boys than with me."

"Does he do that a lot? Go out with the boys and leave you home?"

"I don't know, I guess. I mean, I go, but it ain't the same. Like on my birthday. We was supposed to go to a fancy dinner and he ended up dragging me along to go out shootin' cans. I told him that waddn't what I wanted to do, but you think he cared?" She sniveled. "Then he got really mad at me when I told him he shouldn't'a shot that stork."

Shot a stork? "What do you mean? He shot a stork? You mean a big bird?"

"Yeah," she shrugged as if this was a common thing and I was too stupid to know it. "And when I said so, he told me to shut up or he'd shoot my Piddles. That waddn't nice."

"No, Sandy, that wasn't very nice." She was breaking my heart.

But the stork... "Well, happy birthday. What day was it?"

"March twenty-second."

"I hope you have a better one next year. You deserve it."

She stood a little taller, pulled back her shoulders. "I do. And you know what? I ain't taking no sloppy seconds from Earl no more."

"Good for you."

We left the ladies room and found Earl and Dalton waiting at a table, each with a bottle of beer in their hands.

Sandy said to Earl, "I wanna go home."

He shrugged. "Whatever."

Once we got there, they must have made up in record time because the same sounds could be heard from his bedroom. What she saw in him, I could not understand.

Dalton took me by the arm, trying to get me to go out on the porch with him. "We need to talk."

Sandy's voice echoed in my head. *Sometimes he ain't so nice.*

"Not tonight," I said, and eased from his grasp.

He took my arm again, gently. "C'mon."

Fine. I nodded and followed him out to the porch.

The moonlight sparkled on the bayou, revealing tiny ripples on the surface.

Dalton wrapped his arms around me. "I love you. But I don't understand you."

"Yeah," I sighed. "What else is new?"

I pulled from his embrace, went back inside and plopped down on my cot, snuggled Piddles close, and stuck my fingers in my ears.

Chapter Four

Morning couldn't come quickly enough. I was the first up and got the coffee brewing. As Dalton crawled off the couch, I met him with a cup, holding it out for him. It was a peace offering.

"You're the best," he said, one eye open. We made our way out onto the porch and kept our voices low.

"I need to check on something, a hunch," I said. "Something Sandy said last night. It won't take me long."

"You're not going to tell me what it is?"

"Because we are always so honest with each other?" I said with a little too much snark.

He stared, mouth agape.

Ugh. Why do I do that? And I just tried to smooth things over. "Just give me a couple hours this morning."

"Uh-huh."

I set out in the fishing boat without looking back. I'd have to deal with Dalton later. Whatever was going on between us wasn't going to get resolved overnight.

I dialed Greg, our computer wizard back at headquarters.

He answered after one ring. "Yo."

"Yo to you."

"What's up?"

"Would you please check Louisiana DMV for a Sandy someone? Birthday is March twenty-second. She's probably about my age."

The sound of fingers clicking on a keyboard reverberated through my phone. "Sandra Davidson, that sound right?"

He sent her picture to my phone.

"Yep, that's her. Earl's girlfriend. She have a rap sheet?"

"Nothing comes up."

"Okay, can you do a search, see if anything was reported on that date? Any kind of illegal poaching or any reports from this or surrounding counties?"

"Parishes."

"What?"

"Parishes. Louisiana doesn't have counties. They're parishes."

"Right. Can you do a search then and—"

"You mean use Google?"

"Snark noted. Give me a break. I'm in the middle of a swamp here."

"Okay, fine. I got your back. Cuz that's how we roll. Stand by." The click-click-click of his keyboard echoed across the airwaves. "Well, here's something interesting. On March twenty-second, a whooping crane was shot. The carcass was found and reported, but no suspect."

"Ah ha! I knew it." *Gotcha you son of a bitch.* "Whooping cranes are an endangered species. That's a federal crime. Anyone I can talk to about it?"

"Well, it was a tagged bird from the Louisiana

Whooping Crane Research Center. Looks like a lady named Sara McAllister is in charge."

"Greg, you've made my day. I'm going to nail this bastard. He might get off for his other crimes, with this ridiculous plea deal, but shooting a whooping crane—ha! I'm gonna nail him for that. Send me the address."

"Easy does it there. You know how you can get all fired up."

My teeth clenched down hard. *Not from you, too.* "Yeah, well, thanks for the info," I spat out and hung up.

What is it with everyone lately?

I sped toward the boat ramp, ditched the boat, and switched to the car. Certainly there was a god because the air conditioning was working. I flipped the switch to full blast.

With Siri's help, I tracked down Sara McAllister at the White Lake Wetlands Conservation Area, about an hour or so drive away, and she agreed to meet with me.

Very quickly, I realized I'd misjudged the route it would take to get there. There was no direct highway and I found myself bumping down uneven roads lined by canals. As far as I could see, wet fields covered the countryside with floats at even intervals, a white egret perched atop every third one. I was in crawfish country. Flocks of red-winged blackbirds would take flight as I approached, only to land again once I'd passed. Whenever a drainage culvert poked out into a ditch, a turtle or two would be half out of the water next to it, soaking in the sun.

Since I had time, and, remarkably, cell service, I called to check on Chris. He answered right away.

"Hey, have you planned your flight here yet?"

"Um, no. I will."

"Yes, you will."

The line went quiet.

"You there?"

"Yeah."

"What's going on with you, Chris? I'm worried."

"Nothing. Really. I'm fine. How's Dalton?"

"Dalton is Dalton. He's still being all evasive about Africa. It's starting to really piss me off actually."

"I bet."

"I mean, I'm not a damn child."

"Right."

"Dammit, you did it again?"

"Did what?"

"Changed the subject to me so you don't have to talk about what's going on with you."

"There's nothing going on with me."

"Uh-huh."

"Sounds like Dalton is just trying to protect you."

"I know. That's what pisses me off."

"Isn't that what you do when you love someone, take care of them?"

"No." I sighed. "At least I don't think so. I mean, no."

"Oh. Okay."

"You're not helping."

"Sorry."

"I just don't want to be treated that way."

"Okay."

"I don't know what to do."

"Well, I don't know what to tell you."

Something about those words, the way he said them, made the floor fall out from under me. "What do you mean? You always make me feel better."

"Well, sorry. I just don't have it in me today. I got my own shit to deal with."

"I know. I've been trying to—" The line was dead.

I pulled over to the side of the road and put my head down on the steering wheel. Chris was my best friend and I didn't know what to say to make him feel better. Worse, I didn't think he wanted me to say anything at all. I felt useless.

And I still didn't know what to do about Dalton.

For a moment, I thought to call my mom, but she'd just make things worse. She always made things worse.

Nope. I'd figure this out. Somehow.

I slid the gearshift into drive and pulled back into the road.

For miles, I drove past farm after farm of crawfish ponds, counting white birds. Egrets. It seemed like they were perched there with their own private supply of crawfish. "I'm surprised the farmers don't shoot them," I said aloud. Then realized, *of course they do.* Some of them. Even though it's short-sighted and illegal.

Not much of a step to shooting a whooping crane. *Damn Earl.*

Something else niggled at me.

I called Greg again.

"Yo."

"Yo. One more thing."

"I'm at your service, my liege."

"Oh for poop's sake."

"Just saying I'm sorry."

"Okay, whatever. Can you just check something else for me? Sandy mentioned her job. Something about Earl only wanting her for her job."

"Sure. Standby." Click click click. "She works for the U.S. postal service."

"Hm."

"Great bennies. Federal job, pension, health care."

"Yeah, good point. If they were married."

"From what I understand, all you need is an Elvis."

"Another good point."

"Anything else?"

"Yeah. Earl's friend Al has a nice pond full of alligator snapping turtles." I tried to give a general location of his place. "See if you can find anything on him."

Click click click.

"Yep. Someone called in an anonymous tip about his turtles. He's on a watch list."

"Anything come of it?"

"He's on a list."

"Right. Thanks."

So many lists. And not enough time to follow up.

I got to the parking lot of the White Lake Wetlands Conservation Area early, so I decided to take a stroll on the nature trail to dispense with some nervous energy. I had too much going on in my head.

The air was thick with the odor of rotting vegetation and the buzz of insects. I lingered in the shade of a small pavilion where there was a nice kiosk with all kinds of information on the local flora and fauna, including the whooping cranes. I knew they were one of the world's most endangered birds, but I had no idea how big they were—about the height of an average human, nearly five feet tall, with a wingspan of over seven feet. Most fascinating is their five-foot long trachea that allows them to make their signature whoop that can be heard at long distances.

Seeing one here at the refuge was possible, though very unlikely. As I walked, I kept scanning the area for the distinctive birds with their bright, white plumage, black wing tips, and glorious crimson crown. About fifty feet from the kiosk, three birds lifted from the grass—white with black wing tips. I drew in a breath. Then exhaled. False alarm. They had curved bills and were too small. White ibis.

A little farther down the trail, I spotted an alligator sunning in the mud, its eyes closed. As I approached, the outer eyelid slowly opened, then the inner, transparent, nictitating membrane slid across the eye and the gator fixed his gaze on me, bringing me to a halt. I had to admit, large reptiles gave me pause. If he wanted to, he could lunge at me in a thirty mile-per-hour burst. I wouldn't have a chance. But this guy had seen many humans on this trail before, and he lazily closed his eyes again, dismissing me.

A Double-crested Cormorant perched on a dead tree, staring off into the distance. I wondered what he saw out there that I couldn't.

Warblers flitted through the bushes while one Great Kiskadee squawked from a treetop. I stopped on the short bridge that spanned the drainage ditch. Three turtles had hauled out onto a mud spit, the same species Earl had been selling when he got caught—Red-eared Sliders. In the past, baby Red-eared Sliders were sold in pet stores all over the United States, and I could see why they were so popular, with their beautiful markings.

From there, I took my time, moseying around the first, short loop. That's when the doubt set in. What was I doing here? The odds of connecting Earl to the shooting of a whooping crane that happened months ago were slim. No, impossible. Not to mention, Hyland would string me up for spending time on it. I was on a pointless mission. A tangent, she'd call it. A meaningless waste of time.

As I rounded the corner, heading back toward the bridge, I saw an all-terrain vehicle pull into the parking lot. I assumed it was Sara.

Well, it wasn't meaningless to me.

As I walked toward her, she strode toward me, removing work gloves to shake my hand.

She looked me in the eye as she shook my hand and struck me as a straight-shooting kind of woman. No pretense. What you see is what you get.

I showed her my badge. "Thanks so much for talking with me," I said, noticing the fresh mud on her knee-high rubber boots. "I'm sorry to take you from your work."

"Let's talk in the shade, shall we?"

"Sounds like a lovely idea," I said, wiping sweat from my brow.

She led me to a pavilion and we sat across from each other at a picnic table. "How can I help?"

"I understand that one of your cranes was found shot earlier this year. March twenty-second to be exact."

She nodded. "Unfortunately, that's not all that uncommon."

"I think I know who did it."

Her eyebrows raised. "Really? Well, I admit, I never expected anyone to say that."

"Problem is, the guy's currently working with us on a case. I work on the Presidential Animal Task Force, so it's complicated. His involvement could lead us to information about a much bigger case. Anyway, because of it, he's been given a plea deal. But shooting an endangered species isn't listed as a crime of which he could be exonerated."

"I don't follow."

"I have a credible witness, possibly others. So, once he gives us what we need for our case, I want to arrest him for shooting the crane. Violating the Endangered Species Act can get him up to a year in jail and a $50,000 fine."

"Yeah, well, that would be great." She didn't seem all that enthused by my declaration.

"I don't understand. Don't you care?"

"Of course I care. And maybe, being who you are, you'll be able to do it." She sat back and let her shoulders slump. "It's just that nine whoopers have been shot and killed in Louisiana since 2011. No one has received that kind of sentence or fine. Not even close. So, forgive me, but I guess I'll believe it when I see it."

I nodded in understanding. "Well, I intend to fight for it. This guy's a real dirtbag."

"Well, that doesn't surprise me either. I wish I understood why people shoot 'em," she said, shaking her head. "In our experience, they're not hunters mistaking them for game birds, or some other semi-understandable excuse. Just some people use wildlife for target practice. For kicks."

"Sometimes it's worse."

"Do I even want to know?" she said.

I shook my head. "I assume you have the needed information: where the bird was found, approximate time of death, cause of death."

"We do. But you knew that before you came out here. We filed the report."

"Yes. I was hoping you might have some other information."

She paused. "Like what?"

She wasn't trying to be difficult. It was the response of someone who'd learned not to get her hopes up.

"Like…" I sighed. *Dammit.* "You're right. I got nothing. I was going out of a limb." I looked out over the grassy wetlands. "Sometimes my colleagues say I'm too optimistic."

"That's a bad thing?"

I swung back to meet her gaze and grinned. "Yeah, apparently."

"You're young. You're supposed to be optimistic. Being

jaded doesn't hit until at least your thirties. Then cynicism around fifty. They say by the time your eighty, you don't give a shit about just about anything."

I laughed out loud.

"If you ask me, we could all use a little more optimism."

I couldn't help but smile. "I guess I can admit I needed a break from duty, from dealing with the dirtbags, and this seemed like a nice one. I actually thought I might get to see a whooper while I was here."

She placed her hands on the picnic table and pushed herself to her feet. "Well, if that's the case, let's make it happen."

I stared up at her. "Are you serious?"

"Sure, you've earned an inside look, haven't you? I mean, you fight for wildlife every day, right?"

I didn't know what to say.

"Unless that badge was a fake."

"No, no." I pushed up from the seat. "I'd love it."

I followed her to an aluminum skiff and climbed aboard after her.

She put it into gear and it purred as we took off. "We have a few top-netted pens where the cranes are cared for until release, not far down the canal."

Little butterflies of excitement tickled my stomach as the skiff glided through the muddy water. Once at the dock, I nearly skipped toward the pen trying to hide my excitement. I didn't have the boots to slosh through the wetland, but I didn't care. I wanted to see a whooper.

As she'd said, the pen had tall fencing surrounding a wet area and a net across the top so the birds couldn't fly out.

Inside were three adolescent cranes—white with buffy-brown patches—and two people dressed in white costumes that covered their heads.

"They're completely covered so the birds don't imprint on humans," Sara said. "We're trying to prepare them for reintroduction. They've been raised since chicks that way. The handlers feed them with crane-head hand puppets."

"Are they feeding them now?"

"No, just checking on them today. They're big enough to feed themselves now. I'm sorry we don't have a release planned today. That's always a joy to see."

"I bet," I said. "It must be bittersweet though. I'm sure you must worry about them."

"I do. But it does no good. We can't protect them forever. We raise them to be self-sufficient, as best we can, and we set them free, to live as natural a life as possible. To survive and thrive, they've got to make their own decisions."

"That's a beautiful thought," I said. *Make their own decisions. If only Dalton saw things the same way.*

That's how all adults should be treated—respectfully allowed to make their own decisions. What did it say about someone, about a relationship, when one didn't trust the other enough to treat them like an adult? I knew the answer. It wasn't a good one.

"Are you all right?" Sara stared at me.

"What? Oh yeah. Just…yeah."

One bird made a little hop, its wings outstretched, while another pecked at the dry marsh grass floating in the water. They both had leg bands above their knees.

"They're magnificent," I said. "The way they strut. They act like royalty."

She grinned. "I've never heard it expressed that way before, but yes, I see what you mean."

I pictured a crane flying overhead, its wings spread

wide, soaring on the wind, and then there was Earl, squeezing the trigger, knocking it out of the sky. Rage rumbled in my gut.

"Thank you," I said and turned back toward the boat. "I could stay all day and watch these birds, but I am taking you away from your job. I appreciate the peek."

"Okay then," she said, following me. As we got back into the skiff, she said, "You'll let me know then, about the shooter?"

"I will."

"And I hope you work out the other issue."

I turned to her. "The other issue?"

"The one that brought you all the way out here. The reason you needed a break." Her eyes were filled with genuine concern.

"Oh that. Yes." I nodded, embarrassed I'd shared too much. "That one is…" I looked down at my hands. "Thank you. You're very kind."

As I raised my gaze to meet hers, her warm smile gave me an unexpected comfort.

"Things have a way of working out," she said.

"Yeah, I'm sure you're right," I said. But I wasn't.

Back at the parking area, I thanked her again, turned to go, but something made me turn back. "How do you do it? Knowing the odds? How do you stay optimistic when, well, maybe you're not making a difference at all?"

A gentle smile spread across her face. "Of course I'm making a difference," she said. "And so are you, my dear. Just because you can't see it, doesn't mean it's not true."

I didn't know how to respond, and simply stood there with a dumb look on my face. She gave me a wave. I got into the car and headed toward the fish camp. Part of me wanted to call Hyland, but I knew better. I'd learned. She'd tell me the crane incident wasn't relevant, to stay the course. So I would do that, and I'd wait until the right moment, and then I was going to nail him.

I glanced down at my cell phone on the seat next to me. *Nope, I'm not gonna call her.* The darn thing rang. Startled, I sucked in my breath. It was Dalton.

"I need you back here right away. The exporter made contact. Earl's got a meet-up scheduled."

Chapter Five

Apparently, while I was away, Earl had received an email on an account that he had set up just to receive inquiries like this. It didn't make any sense to me, how the buyer would find him that way, how the behind-the-scenes technology worked, but it didn't matter now. He had a meeting. That's what was important. Soon, we'd be rid of him, and his obnoxious tee-hee-heeing, and chasing the exporter instead.

The email read: Let's meet in person. I have an offer that I don't want to put in writing. I'm sure you understand.

"Does he always contact you via email?" I asked.

"No," said Earl. "It's all, kinda, different ways. Sometimes he texts me. Sometimes, I don't know, like a letter, or somethin'."

"So how do you know it's him?"

"'Cause it is."

"Okay then," Dalton interrupted. "Let's write him back and get the details of when and where."

The reply came immediately. Earl was supposed to

meet him in New Orleans, down in the French Quarter, in Jackson Park, by the famous coffee and beignet shop, Café du Monde. Earl was instructed to wear a red shirt, sit on a bench, and wait.

It seemed like an odd choice, but maybe he wanted the crowds to blend in to, to be able to check Earl out before he met with him, to make sure he wasn't followed or someone was with him.

Dalton thought this was an acceptable location. It made it easier to mix into the crowd and keep an eye on Earl.

Fine. We'd go about this the old-fashioned way, eyes on the street. We'd blend in.

"So what does he look like?" I asked Earl.

"Well, I don't know."

"What do you mean you don't know? You told us you've been selling to this guy for a long time."

"Oh, I have. Yeah, I have. I jus' nevva met him though."

Hadn't Earl said he sold to this guy in person before? Or maybe his testimony had been that he just knew about the guy. I'd have to go back and check for sure.

"So, how did you hook up with him to begin with?" Dalton asked.

"I jus' knew he was da guy, you know. Everybody 'round here sells ta him. Ya know, people talk. And you jus' let 'em know ya got stuff ta sell and it happens, ya know what I mean?"

I'd heard this kind of explanation before. It's what drug dealers always say when asked about finding users. They claim they just show up with money. And it does make sense. If those people are addicts, they'll work really hard to find a source of drugs. These guys weren't much different. Turtles were easy to find. They just had to exchange them for what they wanted—money.

"What do we need to know going into this meeting?" Dalton asked.

Earl shrugged.

"Come on now, you've got to help us out a little bit more than that."

"I don' know, man."

I stepped toward him. "Well, you better know, because it's part of our agreement. So start talking."

"Alls I know is what it says dere in dat email. And what da guys say."

Dalton and I waited.

He stared.

I wanted to slug him. "And what do the guys say?"

"Well, you know, ta be real careful, not ta cross him."

Dalton frowned and folded his arms across his chest. "What do you think he wants to talk about in person? It seems pretty risky if he already has a system set up to buy turtles without ever having to get directly involved himself."

Earl mustered another shrug. "How's I supposed to know. I ain't no damn mind reader."

I rolled my eyes. "Well, that's for damn sure."

I walked away. We were getting nowhere.

I motioned for Dalton to follow me. When we were out of earshot, I said, "This jerk isn't helping at all. And I don't trust him. I wish we could put a bug on him, but all it would take is a search and we lose this exporter. He'll be in the wind." I ran my fingers through my hair "Ugh. I hate having to rely on this moron."

"Let's just go with it. Earl might surprise us."

I stared at him for a moment. "You can't be serious."

"We don't have a choice."

"That's more the point."

"Whatever."

"Well, I don't like it. I don't like it one bit."

Dalton said, "Noted. But sometimes, when building relationships, we gotta do things we don't like."

I shifted back on my heels. "Yeah? Maybe you should take some of your own advice."

It was two o'clock on a Saturday and the artists and other vendors were set up on the sidewalk surrounding the park. Tarot card readers, palm readers, street musicians and oil painters. There was even a guy doing a juggling act as a small, impromptu audience gathered around. I had to give it to him, the guy really knew how to work a crowd.

Dalton and I had established a perimeter. Dalton patrolled the river side; I patrolled the other side.

I mingled through the booths, keeping my eye on the bench where Earl sat twiddling his thumbs. He kept looking at his watch. *Stop that Earl. Be patient. Don't look like you're going to bolt at any second.*

I looked all the way across the park, but I couldn't spot Dalton anywhere. That man sure did know how to be invisible. He had come to this job with all his training from being a Navy SEAL. And he was damn good at it. I, on the other hand, had none. Sure, I'd been top of my class at FLETCE, but had no practical experience. In fact, I was still in my first six months on the job, a probationary time-frame, when I'd been reassigned to work undercover with Dalton. He didn't like it then, but he'd come to respect my abilities. At least I'd thought he had. But now, keeping information from me about my own father's death was not acceptable. Who was he to decide what I could handle and what I couldn't?

I had to keep my mind in the game. I circled back, moseying through a stall of paintings that were displayed in such a way that I could look through the chicken wire they were hung on as the clock tick-tocked, tick-tocked.

What if this was all a farce? How did we know there was a real person coming? Earl could've made the whole thing up. Was he that stupid? He had to know that to get out of his conviction, he had to give up a bigger fish. He couldn't keep us on the hook forever.

Well, he was pretty stupid. We'd see.

Earl stood up. I froze in place. Watched. What was he doing? He stretched, lifted his arms up over his head, stretched some more, and then slowly sat back down. What was that? Was he motioning someone off? Was it some kind of signal?

I glanced around. There wasn't anyone looking at him that I could see. What was he up to?

Maybe he truly was too stupid to realize that if he didn't actually come through and give up the buyer, he was still going to jail. I made a mental note to explain that to him later.

The minutes ticked by while I pretended to admire some more paintings.

Then someone caught my attention, heading right toward Earl. *Oh no.* Sandy.

What was she doing here? What were the odds? Had he signaled her?

She threw her hands up. He shook his head. I forced myself to keep my feet planted where they were. He had to get rid of her.

Her hands balled into fists and landed on her hips as she came to a halt in front of him.

Earl wouldn't look her in the eye. He kept glancing around to see if anyone was looking.

I scanned the crowd. No one stared in their direction.

Finally Earl stood up, leaned in, and whispered in her ear. She huffed and stormed off.

What was that all about?

Hopefully, if the buyer had seen, he wouldn't be spooked.

I glanced at the time on my phone. Dalton and I had agreed that at certain intervals we would pass, and switch sides so as not to gather attention to ourselves loitering about. I headed for the crossover location. As I passed Dalton, he made a slight shake of his head. I did the same. I hadn't seen anything suspicious or out of the ordinary.

On the other side of the park, along the main thoroughfare, horse drawn carriages were lined up, one after the other, the carriage drivers hawking for passengers. I stopped to look at one particular horse that caught my eye. The driver was a woman and she had painted the horse's hooves with toenail polish. A bright pink with sparkles. I had to admit, it was an attention grabber.

"You like a ride?" she asked.

I stopped and asked her about the polish, making sure I was facing Earl so I could see anything that was happening while we chatted. She told me the horse's name was Polly, and that she loved to be groomed and have her hooves polished. I was sure it was all a story made to help her stand out. She claimed she had a happy horse, willing to pull any tourist around the streets. Who was I to judge? I looked the horse over and she seemed healthy.

As I moved on, something caught my eye. Someone on the other side of the park, shifting from one foot to the other, looking at Earl and looking away. I moved in. He had his back turned to me, but I was sure he was eyeing Earl.

This was it. This was the guy. My heartbeat ramped up speed.

I moved around the exterior circle of the park, staying behind some bushes. I couldn't let him see me.

Then he turned and looked right in my direction. I jumped back as if he'd smacked me with a hot coal. It was Kevin. *Holy crap!* It was Kevin. Australian Kevin. From Costa Rica. Here in New Orleans.

I'll be damned. He's the exporter.

Chapter Six

There was no question that he was the exporter. Kevin had been in Costa Rica when I was called down to help Dalton with an op there. He was one of the other buyers. I'd even gone to talk to him on my own.

A rush of excitement flooded my body. Earl really had come through. I even knew exactly what this guy looked like, and we could take it from here. A grin crept across my face. No more having to deal with Earl.

Kevin shifted from one foot to the other, scanning the area. I suddenly remembered that he could recognize me as well. I couldn't let him see me. I chewed on my thumb. Now I had to think fast; this wasn't just a typical surveillance situation. He would recognize me or Dalton right away, and could bolt.

Kevin sauntered toward Earl, appearing to walk casually about, taking in his surroundings. He came to a stop and reached for something in his pocket. A pack of cigarettes. He took one out and held it to his mouth. As he used a match to light it, he took the opportunity to look around again.

He was definitely alert and aware. Why? If Earl was a local yokel, just selling a couple of turtles, why all the concern? They weren't making a transaction right now. Nothing illegal. Just a conversation, according to Earl.

Kevin continued onward, but when he got to Earl he passed right by. From where I could see, no words were exchanged, nothing was said, not even a glance. In fact, Earl didn't seem to recognize him at all.

At least that matched what Earl claimed. Regardless, there he was. Whether he decided to make contact with Earl or not didn't matter. There was no doubt in my mind —Kevin was the exporter.

I moved along the sidewalk to stay parallel with him as he moved out of the park. I wasn't going to lose him now. Greg had already checked on the email, and confirmed there was no way to track him electronically. I had to follow him now, and if I lost him, it was over.

When he got to the street, he hung a left, heading past Café Du Monde, and continued down the sidewalk. I tried to stay among the tourists, moving side to side, ducking low whenever he looked over his shoulder.

I never took my eyes off of him as I pulled my phone from my pocket and called Dalton. "I've got him. It's Kevin from Costa Rica. Did you see him?"

"What? Are you serious?"

"Dead serious. Yes. Stay with Earl. I'm tailing him now."

"Roger that. Be careful."

I wasn't sure what I would do if Kevin saw me, but I knew I had to track him. I couldn't make an arrest. He hadn't done anything. But this was my only chance or he might be in the wind. Maybe I could find out where he was staying or anything that might be helpful. Until we could set up official surveillance.

He continued down Decatur Street, then suddenly crossed to the south side. I started across as well and a giant, red, double-decker bus blared the horn. I'd nearly stepped out in front of it. With my heart racing out of control, I looked both ways before crossing to continue following him. At Dumaine Street, he crossed at the light, heading north again. I skipped across the intersection kitty-corner to keep up.

One block down, the music of a second line parade reverberated off the buildings. Kevin caught up with them and seemed to meld into the group. I caught the tail end of the parade, strutting along with the mourners, clapping my hands and stepping to the beat. The tuba blasted out a melody while someone blew into a whistle—a peppy, syncopated beat. A trumpet joined in, countering the tuba.

I moved through the brightly-colored parasols, trying to keep up. When the parade turned left on Royal Street, Kevin popped out from the crowd and continued down Dumaine Street. There weren't many people on the sidewalk. I was sure it was a ploy to see who might follow. So I hung back among the parasols as long as I could. At the next intersection, Bourbon Street, he hung a right. It was too risky to stay that close behind him with too few people to hide among.

I headed down Royal Street, walking parallel with him. One block over, at St. Philip Street, I caught sight of him again. He was heading back my way. There was no doubt, he was walking a path to be sure he wasn't followed. I ducked into The Red Truck Gallery and lingered by the window, waiting for him to walk by. When he did, I slipped back through the door and followed once again. He stayed on St. Philip Street all the way back to North Peters Street.

Was he headed down to the station to get on the street car? If he did and it wasn't jam-packed with people, I'd have to decide to get on or not. If he recognized me, it would be game over.

He made a quick glance over his shoulder before heading into the French Market. He was no idiot. The market gave him an opportunity to see if anyone had followed. I had to be very cautious.

He went in through the arched entryway, where two palm trees grew in huge terra-cotta pots on either side.

I waited as long as I could, maybe thirty seconds, before I followed him in.

I needed a moment for my eyes to adjust from the bright sunshine outside to the dark hallway. It was packed with people. Stall after stall overflowed with fresh produce, ice cream, coffee, even grilled gator sausage on a stick.

To the left were carts loaded with arts and crafts by local artisans. I moved with a crowd of tourists, past the shrimp Creole sauce shop and a café selling breakfast all day.

I didn't see Kevin anywhere so I picked up the pace. He couldn't have gone far. He wasn't in the oyster bar, or at the banana smoothie shack. I pushed onward amid the throngs.

As I moved through, I checked in each store. No Kevin. Then I was at the last stall and burst out onto the street at the Louisiana State Museum. I looked left, then right. Still, no Kevin. Where had he gone? I circled back, rushed through the market, then spun around and went back through again.

Dammit!

He had vanished.

Chapter Seven

I called Dalton back. "I lost him. I can't believe it. I lost him."

"Which way? Maybe I can pick him up?"

"No, he's just gone."

"Well, where are you now?"

"I'm at the French Market. I'll head back toward you. I can't believe it was Kevin. What's he doing here in Louisiana anyway? He's Australian, and he was buying in Costa Rica. Now he's here?"

"I don't see how that matters. Where there's money to be made, people come from anywhere."

"I guess you're right. I'll be right there." I hung up.

What was I going to tell Hyland? *Hey sorry, I had him in my sights and lost him.*

When I got to Dalton, he had Earl standing down by the river where we could keep an eye on him while we talked without him hearing us.

"What did Earl say?" I asked.

"Nothing. And I believe him. He never saw the guy. I think he's genuinely clueless."

"Of course he's genuinely clueless." I threw up my hands in frustration. "That's the definition of an idiot."

"Okay, let's both take a deep breath here. We got some information, let's work with it. You're sure it was Kevin from Costa Rica?"

I nodded. "There's no doubt in my mind. It was him."

"And he didn't see you?"

I shook my head. "I don't think so. I mean, I followed protocol."

He nodded with reassurance.

"But Hyland isn't going to be very happy with me."

"Let's worry about that when we have to. First things first. We need to find out why he didn't actually make contact with Earl. Maybe he saw me. Or it's possible he saw you before you even saw him. If I were in his shoes, I would've taken off, too."

"And there's no question," I said, "he was doing everything he could to make sure *he* wasn't being followed."

Dalton put his hands on his hips. "I don't know what to think of all this." He looked around, his finger tapping on his jeans. Finally he said, "Let's have Earl email him back, ask him why he didn't show up. Maybe he'll actually answer, especially if he thinks it's a secure connection. It's a long shot, but you never know. If he wants to buy turtles, he has to connect with someone."

Earl left his position and headed our way. "Hey man, I gotta take a piss."

Dalton frowned. "Get your ass back over there and stay where I told you."

Earl turned tail and went back where he was told.

"Wow, so you're finally getting a little frustrated too, huh?"

"Who said I wasn't before?"

"You didn't seem to—"

"After you left this morning, he and Sandy were at it again. He was bragging about the size of his package."

"Yeah, I just threw up in my mouth."

"Just be glad you weren't there."

That made me smile. "I guess we're not accomplishing anything standing around here anymore."

"Agreed. Might as well let the guy go to the bathroom."

"You know, I am enjoying the breeze off the river. We could stay a little while longer."

Dalton grinned. "You're evil."

When we got back to Earl's fish camp, Piddles was there to greet us, yapping at our feet and dancing around in circles. Earl scowled. He hooked his foot under the dog's belly and flipped him into the water. The little dog let out a mid-air yelp before he submerged, then popped up squeaking and sputtering.

My rage hit a fever pitch. "Hey, pick on someone your own size!"

"Huh?" he grumbled, heading for the refrigerator.

I grabbed his arm. "I'm serious. Knock it off."

He swung around to face me. "Yeah? Ya gonna make me?"

"If I have to." God this guy was pissing me off. He reached toward me, to put his hand on my shoulder. I grabbed a hold of his wrist, pinned his thumb into a thumb hold, and twisted him to his knees.

He let out a shriek. "What da hell, woman?"

"Yeah, what the hell is right. When I say knock it off, I mean knock it off."

He looked at Dalton.

Dalton said, "Dude, you're on your own, man. Haven't you learned yet not to piss her off?"

Earl shook his head and I let go.

"Now get the dog."

"Screw dat," he said as he grabbed a broom. He scooped Piddles out of the swamp. The little dog shook off the water and scampered into the bedroom. Earl tossed the broom in the corner. "I'm goin' fishing."

"Sure," said Dalton. "But in the rowboat, and right out there"—he pointed with his finger—"right where we can see you and no further."

"You gotta be shittin' me?"

"Do I look like I'm kidding?"

"Hey, I held up my end of da damn deal. I got ya buyer. Ya need ta lay the hell off."

Dalton's expression changed, ever so slightly. He didn't say a word, simply scowled.

Earl's shoulders slumped. He took three beers from the refrigerator, grabbed his fishing pole, plopped down into the row boat, and rowed out to the middle of the river.

"That's not nearly far enough," I said to Dalton. "Antarctica would be better."

Dalton smirked.

"For us I mean. He can stay here in this wretched heat."

I poured a couple of iced teas and we sat down in the lawn chairs where we could keep an eye on Earl and talk.

"None of this makes sense," I said. "When you think about it, we've got an exporter who's obviously Australian, at least he has a very heavy Australian accent, who very recently was trying to buy in Costa Rica. By a huge coincidence, he now happens to be here, trying to buy turtles in Louisiana, to then transport and sell in China or Japan."

"I'm not sure any of that matters," Dalton said. "People go where the money is. Turtles are big business right now."

It was true. Demand for turtles in Asia had skyrocketed in the last few years. Their own native wood turtle is nearly extinct, therefore, many North American species are filling the demand. One of the driving factors is that in China, there are four revered creatures. Three of them are fictional—the Dragon, the Phoenix, and the white tiger. The fourth one is the tortoise. And so it's thought to be very good luck to have a pet turtle. With the increase in wealth in that region, they are in greater demand, therefore traffickers can get a higher price, making them even more coveted. Wood turtles sell for up to $1,700 each.

Due to that demand, freshwater turtles are especially vulnerable to overexploitation and are now among the world's most endangered vertebrates. For most turtle species, only about two percent of hatchlings reach adulthood. Since they take so long to sexually mature, every adult turtle taken from the wild significantly reduces the reproduction rate.

Which only makes them more in demand.

Earl hollered from the rowboat, "Hey, man, bring me out some more beer."

I raised my middle finger.

The buzz of an outboard engine coming down the river made him turn to look in that direction. Soon it was clear who was coming our way. Earl's buddy, Al, was at the wheel of a speed boat, Sandy at his side. As they approached, the boat slowed. Sandy saw Earl out in the rowboat and then looked back at us, confused. Al brought the boat up to the fish camp shack and cut the engine.

"I jus' came out ta git Piddles," Sandy said. The dog yipped and spun around with excitement.

Earl had turned his rowboat toward us and was rowing with a vengeance. "What da hell, woman!" he shouted.

"You wit Al now? Well, ain't dat jus' rich. Go on ahead den, you dumb dog-lovin' slut."

"I will," she shrieked. "He knows how ta treat a lady. Unlike you!"

Al sat back in the boat's driver's seat, saying nothing.

"Well, screw ya both den," Earl said.

Sandy scooped up her dog in her arms and plopped down in the boat seat next to Al.

Al started up the engine.

"Piss off," Earl yelled over the engine and turned his back on them.

I leaned toward Dalton and whispered, "What a jackass. Got what he deserved."

Dalton nodded. "He's going to be a real pain in the ass now."

"If only we could duct tape *him* up and ship him off to China."

Chapter Eight

Earl was passed out on the couch. His phone beeped and Dalton fumbled for it in his pocket. Earl looked up at him, his eyes glazed over. But as Dalton pulled away, Earl clamped his hand down on Dalton's wrist.

"Dude, you got a text," Dalton said and held the phone so Earl could see the screen.

He bolted upright. "Hey, I think it's him."

"What do you mean?" Dalton flipped the phone over to look for himself.

"Da guy. On my phone. He's textin' me."

"How do you know it's him?"

"I tol' you. He switches it up. But it's him jus' the same."

I moved to look over Dalton's shoulder at the screen. Sure enough, it was a note from Kevin: We were supposed to meet at the park. Alone. What are you trying to pull?

"Dammit! I knew it. He saw us," I said to Dalton. "He saw me."

"Or maybe he's just paranoid. He doesn't say anything specific."

"No, he saw me."

Dalton touched my wrist. "It could've been me."

"It was me. With my red hair. Of course it would be me. And I'm the one who followed him."

"Let's not beat ourselves up. We had no idea it would be someone who would recognize us."

"Still."

Dalton thought a moment. "Maybe we can use this to our advantage. He thinks we're also buyers, right?"

"Yeah, if our covers are intact. But wouldn't he find the coincidence just as fishy as we do?"

We stared at each other, trying to figure out what to do.

Dalton finally said, "Let's see if we can figure out what he saw, what he thinks he knows."

"I say we act dumb, like Earl."

"Hey!" Earl said, rubbing his forehead.

Dalton typed a reply: Ain't nobody followed me.

"That's perfect," I said.

Earl shook his head and rolled his eyes.

Dalton clicked send.

And we waited.

I poured another glass of iced tea. Then *ding*, a reply came in: You lie. You aint worth my time.

"Well, ya see," Earl said, "ya done gone and messed it up. I delivered the buyer to ya, jus' like we done agreed, and ya went and scared him off."

Dalton and I both turned to glare at him.

Dalton turned back to me. "We need to explain our presence. A supply and demand thing. Let's admit Earl's been approached by other buyers, but he trusts the former arrangement with Kevin."

"Yeah," I said. "Maybe even have him admit they were willing to pay more, but he wants to honor their long-term relationship." I turned my gaze back to Earl. "How would you phrase that?"

"Yeah, no." Earl said, shaking his head. "I don' think he'd go for it neither way. I tol' you, he's squirrelly. He's gonna bolt."

"You said you've been selling to him for quite some time. Certainly there must be some level of trust that—"

"I never said how long."

I could feel my neck turning red. "While at the plea-bargain hearing, you certainly implied that you had a long-standing relationship."

"Yeah, so, we do. I do. He jus' being cautious, dat's all. He prolly saw you, like you said, and he don' want no trouble. Maybe he knows you da feds."

I looked at Dalton. He seemed as frustrated as I was.

"What's it matter no how?" Earl said. "One time or eight hundred, he still what you been lookin' for, ain't he? It ain't my fault. You can't pin dis on me."

I turned back to Dalton. "Can we just kill him now?" I gestured for him to step away so we could talk privately. Earl plopped back down on the couch.

"Okay, why would Kevin say that anyway? Maybe he is on to us? You don't think the Brittany and John Fuller covers are blown, do you?"

Dalton shook his head. "If he knew we were feds, he wouldn't text at all. He'd be a ghost."

"I agree. So we're going on the assumption that he saw one of us and it's simply a competition thing then."

Dalton was thinking.

I offered, "Why don't we say, 'Screw it. I got product coming out of my ears. You want to buy or what?'"

Dalton shrugged. "Why not?" He typed it in and hit send. Then we stared at each other, waiting. I thought to call Greg, and have him trace the number, but Kevin was smart enough to text from a burner phone, and even if we could get a GPS location, he'd be gone as soon as this conversation was over.

A text came back: What's your asking price?

Yes!

Dalton turned back to Earl. "What are the numbers?"

"Wait," I said. "Wouldn't someone like Earl be paranoid himself at this point? I mean, really, Kevin's not the only one who could get in trouble with the law here. Earl could, too. Why don't you say something like, 'How do I know it's you, not a cop?'"

Earl piped up, "I wouldn't say it like that."

"Okay, how would you say it?"

He stared. "Well, I guess I would."

"You guess you would what?"

"Okay, fine, I's sayin' I guess I would say it like dat."

I whispered to Dalton. "When this is over, I swear to God…"

Dalton was already typing. Then he paused and looked up at me. "Are you sure that's what you wanna do?"

"Yeah, why not?"

He shrugged. "I don't know. It just seems like that's what a cop would say to make someone think he's not a cop."

"Oh my god, you've got to be kidding."

"Okay, fine. Let's go with it and see what happens."

"I need a drink." I went to the refrigerator and cracked open an ice cold Budweiser. Not my beer of choice, but it was here, and it was cold. I went out on the porch.

Dalton grabbed a beer for himself and followed me. "We'll get him back, Poppy," he said. "Stop beating yourself up about it." He held the phone in one hand and a cold beer in the other.

"It's not that so much," I said. "It's just that I've been

here too long, with this guy too long. I think I need a vacation."

"So let's take one," Dalton said, grinning at me. "Where do you want to go? Anywhere in the world. Just you and me." He pulled me tight against him, wrapping his arms around me, and gave me a nice long kiss. "I could use a little alone time, too."

"How about Africa?"

He pulled away. "Not this again."

"Why not? You went."

"There's nothing there, Poppy."

"I don't believe you."

"Don't you see what this is doing to our relationship?"

"Don't you? You're the one who chose to go there. Without telling me, I might add."

"I was trying to—" His jaw tightened. "You know what. Forget it."

"Fine."

"Fine."

"And I didn't mean with you anyway."

"What?"

"The vacation. Chris is coming here, and I want a few days off. I'm worried about him and I need a break, too."

Dalton's expression changed. Was he disappointed? "I think that's a good idea," he finally said.

"Really?"

"Really."

"I will then. Just as soon as we nail this guy."

The phone beeped with a new incoming text. Dalton held up the phone and looked at the screen. He flipped it around so I could read the words: No deal.

Crap!

Chapter Nine

I collapsed into the lawn chair. "I suppose we have to call Hyland now."

"I can do it," Dalton said.

"No, I'm the one who lost him. I'll do it." I chugged down the rest of my beer. "Do you think she'll fire me this time?"

"Why would she do that? You did your job, at a significant disadvantage. How could we have known the target could recognize us?" He paused, cocked his head to the side. "Why are you so worried that you're going to be fired?"

"She doesn't like me, that's why. She doesn't even talk to me in complete sentences."

"I'm sure you're reading more into it than is there."

I shook my head. "I don't know."

I pushed myself up and out of the chair and went to get my phone. I punched in her number and listened to it ring, hoping she wouldn't pick up. Then I heard the click of the call connecting, of course.

"Agent McVie. Do you have an update?"

I let out my breath. "I do. The buyer made contact and set up a meet with Earl in a public place. We got eyes on him. Unfortunately, the exporter is a person of interest from a previous operation, and we think he recognized one or both of us."

"Are you saying you're blown?"

"No. Not necessarily. Not as agents. As long as our covers are still intact."

"What operation?"

"Joe's op in Costa Rica, when I was recruited to Special Ops to play Dalton's wife. He was another buyer for the pet trade, at least that's what we assumed at the time."

There was silence while she thought about it. "Can you work that angle? I'll get your IDs reestablished right away."

"We can try, but…"

"But what?"

I could hear the annoyance in her voice. "But once I had visual confirmation, I followed him. He used evasive tactics to lose me."

"Uh-huh."

"He made contact again, via text, but then he bailed."

"I see." More silence. "Do you think he'll try again?"

"I don't know."

"Tell me everything you know about him from Joe's op."

There wasn't much to tell. His name, Australian accent. "Maybe Joe had notes about him in the file, but I had the impression he'd never met him before I arrived in Costa Rica." I sure as hell wasn't going to divulge I'd visited him at his hotel, using the visit as a smoke screen to fool another perp in the operation. Or that there had been an undeniable attraction between us.

"You're sure it's him though? You recognized him?"

"Yes ma'am."

"Send his description to Greg. Have him pull files on all known traffickers, cross reference the description and known locations, and see if we can't get a hit."

"Will do."

"All right then. Carry on." The phone disconnected.

That's it? Carry on? No reprimands? I had the suspect in my sights and I lost him. And she said nothing? Why was she so damn cryptic?

I called Greg and gave him the information. "You realize this will be like finding a needle in a haystack, right?" he said.

"Yeah. But that's what Hyland wants you to do."

He huffed and hung up.

I couldn't stand it anymore. I called Hyland back.

"Yes?" she answered.

"Ma'am, I'm not sure you understood before. I think he saw me. I tailed him, but I lost him. Plain and simple. We had him, right there, and I lost him."

"I understood."

There was a pause.

"I'm not surprised," she said.

Finally. "I know that I don't—"

"Players at that level are very elusive. They never show their faces. I'm impressed you were able to get a look at him and identify him. Good work. We're a step closer."

"Um, thanks."

"Was there something else you needed?"

"Um, no ma'am."

I clicked end and stared at the phone. Yep, I needed a vacation.

I dialed Chris's number. The phone rang twice, then went to voicemail. I'd try him again later.

I sat back down on the chair next to Dalton. "We have to get him back."

"We will. We will," Dalton assured me, though he and I both knew the odds.

"Face it. He's in the wind."

"Maybe. Maybe not. If he has a buyer in Asia, he needs a source for these turtles."

"Yeah, but Earl isn't the only source in this area. There's thousands of turtles and I'm sure hundreds of criminals like Earl willing to sell."

"Exactly," he said. "Maybe we'll get lucky and he'll contact Johnny. We should call Tom and Mike and alert them."

"Sure. You do that. But I need to find him. I need to find him, and I need to fix this."

Dalton sat back, eyed me up and down. "I see that mind working and I don't like it. I know whatever you're going to say next is not going to make me happy and I'll be—"

"We need to resurrect John and Brittany big time. We need to flush him out."

"Oh no. No, no, no, no. This doesn't need to be complicated. We keep it simple. He's going to offer to buy from Earl or Johnny. Then we get a warrant. No undercover shenanigans. No sneaking around, one hand not knowing what the other hand is doing. No, no, nope."

I crossed my arms in front of my chest. "Where is your sense of adventure?"

"You see darlin', that's the thing, I never had one."

"You ran off to Africa. That must have been quite the adventure."

He clenched his teeth together. "That's different and you—" His eyes narrowed. "Why do you have to make things so complicated all the time?"

"I don't. I look at the big picture, and I make things work."

"Yeah, well, yeah, no." He shook his head. "I say we stay the course. We hang out here with Earl, and try to contact him again."

"Great idea. You go ahead." I got up from the chair. "I don't think both of us are needed for that plan."

"Wait. What did Hyland say?"

"She wasn't angry, actually. She told me to have Greg do his thing, so I did. You heard me call him."

"That's it?"

"That's it."

"See, what did I say?"

I turned to face him. "Is that an I-told-you-so?"

"No, I'm just saying. You worry too much. You're doing fine. You're a great agent."

My fists landed on my hips. "You're just saying that because you want to get into my pants."

"I've already been in your pants, and, yes, I want to again, but that's not why I'm saying it. Why can't you believe it?"

"What? That I'm a good agent or that you'd say it?"

"Either."

"Because you're lying."

"What?" He looked incredulous. "Why would you say that?"

"It must be true. Because you don't trust me enough to tell me what you know about my father."

"That's different and you know it." He huffed and turned away.

I gathered my things together and came back out onto the porch with my bag in my hand. "Good luck with Earl. I'm gonna find Kevin." I got into the speedboat and took off before Dalton could stop me.

When I got to the car, I stared out the windshield.

I had no idea where to start.

There was only one person who maybe, possibly, had information that could help. The problem was, he'd retired, and I had no idea how to get a hold of him. I'd need Greg to track him down.

Chapter Ten

Joe Nash was a legend. I had the opportunity to work with him on my very first op when I'd met Dalton, down in Costa Rica. In the end, Joe was happy with the results, he'd even taken me on another op in Alaska, but I was never sure that he had much faith in me. But what did that matter? He had met Kevin, and he might have information that would be helpful.

Greg easily found his phone number. Apparently contact information for all retired personnel is on file. He was now living in The Villages in south Florida.

When I called, he answered right away. "Yeah-low."

"Hi Joe. It's Special Agent Poppy McVie calling. Remember me?"

"Hell yes, I remember you. How are you? What kind of trouble are you in now?" He laughed, a nice low baritone rumble.

"No trouble, sir. How's retirement?"

"Boring as hell. So is getting old. Some advice, never do it."

"Yes sir, I'll work on that." I tapped my finger on the steering wheel.

"Well, pleasantries are nice, God knows I've got all the time in the world for it, but what's on your mind that you've called me? How can I help?"

"Well, sir, I'm in New Orleans. Special Agent Dalton and I have been assigned to babysit a perp who's been selling turtles and—"

"Yeah? How's Dalton anyway? Are you two getting along any better?"

"Uh, yes, sir." *Not really.* "Our directive was to stick with this guy until we could identify his buyer. Well, we made visual contact this morning. And you aren't going to believe this. It was Kevin, the Australian guy from the job in Costa Rica"

"No kidding?"

"I tracked him through the French Quarter, but I lost him, sir. We were able to make contact via text, trying to get him to follow through on the buy, but he got spooked. Now he's in the wind."

"What spooked him?"

"Well, I'm not sure. But he might have seen us. Well, me. Might have seen me."

"When you were tailing him?"

"Or before. We were monitoring a meet."

"And now he's in the wind."

"Exactly."

"So you think I might know something that would help you find him."

"Yes, sir. I was hoping you might have some insight."

"It seems to me, you had some contact with him in Costa Rica as well. And if my hunch was correct, you somehow used him as leverage. Am I right?"

I hesitated. I had gone over the line, actually quite a

ways over the line, to bust the kingpin in Costa Rica. Joe had been willing to look the other way, with an unspoken agreement that I never had to admit it. But now he was retired, so what did it matter? Was he just curious? "I, uh, I guess you could say I created the illusion that there was a bigger, more powerful buyer in town. And I made a little visit to Kevin to show some muscle."

"Are you telling me that you got Maria to crawl out of the woodwork by believing that you were going to buy from someone else? That she'd lose the sales?"

"Yes, sir. That's exactly what I did. I, uh, had a friend of mine, who was visiting, stand in to look like a bigger kingpin. I know it was risky, but when I met Maria, well, my gut told me the way to catch her was to work her ego." I cringed. If I were honest, I was damn lucky the whole scheme didn't fall apart at the first thought.

Joe roared, a rumble that came from the depths of his belly. "Are you kidding me? Dalton and I had been working that case for months. We had no idea Maria was even involved until you showed up. But within a couple days you read the situation and knew it was her. That was brilliant work. I've never seen anything like it. You've got a keen eye and a sharp mind. I bet if you stop and think about it, you already know more about Kevin than you think."

"Well, thank you, sir. I guess, I mean, I think I should head down to the French Quarter and look for him. But…"

"But what?"

"But Special Agent Dalton thinks we should stay the course. He thinks we should wait for Kevin to call again."

"He does, does he? Well, that's why the two of you make a good team—yin and yang. Dalton has a good head on his shoulders. He's a good soldier. I'd have him at my back any day of the week, but he's not going to think out of the box. And that's what it takes in this line of work. Someone who is willing to take a risk. Someone who can outthink the bad guys. Someone who's passionate about the end result. Poppy, all my money is on you. You've got what it takes."

I sat back in the chair. I couldn't believe what I was hearing. Joe Nash, my hero, the person I had admired more than anyone in the field, and made me want to join U.S. Fish and Wildlife's undercover service, was telling me that I had what it takes. I didn't know what to say. My tongue wouldn't move.

"Are you still there?"

"Yes, sir."

"So, you're going to head back to the French Quarter, and you're going to find this guy, and then what? You know he's going to recognize you. And you've got to pull out that old cover, dust it off. Brittany was another buyer. How does that impact the situation? Will you intimidate him and force him to act, like you did with Maria? And then what?"

"I don't know. I don't believe he has the same motivation. Turtles here are a dime a dozen, quite literally. I'm not sure another buyer would cause him to do anything."

"Okay. Then what would?"

"I don't know. I've been racking my brain trying to figure that out."

"Maybe it'll become clear when you find him and you can talk to him."

"Are you serious? Go find him without a plan? And that's assuming I could find him. If he's even there." I slumped with frustration.

"Am I still talking to Special Agent Poppy McVie? The young lady who worked with me in Costa Rica, who flirted her way onto Ray Goldman's boat in Norway, who saved my ass in Alaska? Because that Poppy didn't need a plan.

That exceptional agent flew by the seat of her pants. She knew how to wing it, because she trusted her gut."

Was that what had happened to me? I no longer trusted myself? Is that why I was so frustrated and feeling out of sorts? Had Dalton convinced me to see the world through his eyes? And I'd lost my own perspective?

"Listen, Poppy. You called for my advice about Kevin, but here's a little bit of advice you didn't ask for. Believe in yourself. Trust that gut of yours. And if for some reason, right now, you can't trust that, trust mine. I've worked with a lot of agents over the years, and you've got what it takes. So, whatever is holding you back, let it go. Get out there and make it happen. And when you do, you're going to find yourself in some hairy situations. Times when you've got nothing but your gut. If you hesitate, you're done. Do you hear what I'm saying?"

"I do. I understand. Thank you, sir. I will do just that."

"And as far as finding Kevin, I assume—"

"He had Earl meet him in the French Quarter because he's arrogant, wanted Earl to come to him. That's where he's staying. He either likes the nightlife or the culture or both. Which means if I head down there this evening, I just might be able to find him."

"Exactly. That's my girl. Good luck."

I smiled and let the *girl* comment slide.

Chapter Eleven

It was approaching dinner time when I stepped off the cable car. Did I have time to eat? What I'd give for a nice salad, maybe a glass of wine, check out the foodie scene—I'd never been to New Orleans—but I had to hit the road running. I had a lot of ground to cover, and only a few hours to do it. If Kevin was here, somewhere, I was going to find him.

I remembered the French Quarter Market and the advertised gator-on-a-stick. Who would eat that anyway? No, Kevin wasn't that kind of tourist.

I headed toward Bourbon Street. I wasn't sure it was Kevin's style either. Too far on the side of witless debauchery. He seemed a little more sophisticated, but I'd make one pass through to be sure.

People flocked to the famous street, moving in no particular direction, shoulder to shoulder, monster-sized drinks in their hands. They were mostly coeds, so I fit in. I pushed through the crowd and ducked in and out of each establishment underneath neon signs that displayed the names of bars the likes of The Happy Hooker, Fat Tuesdays, and the famous Cat's Meow. Each had its own vibe—acoustic country music or moody classic rock played under flashing colored lights. I made a quick pass through each, checking the dark corners before heading to the next one.

After twenty minutes, I found myself standing in front of Marie Laveau's House of Voodoo. Little voodoo dolls and talismans hung inside the picture window below a sign for psychic readings. *Maybe I should pop in and see if the psychic knows where Kevin is*. Her guess was as good as mine. But that wasn't true. If I could believe Joe. I had no idea he'd had such faith in me. My head was spinning from his words. I could do this.

Near the end of the strip, I came upon Lafitte's Blacksmith Shop. According to the sign, it was the oldest bar in New Orleans. I'm pretty sure it was just a tourist trap. I made a pass-through. No Kevin.

As I headed for the exit, a guy bumped into me and spilled his beer down the front of himself. I turned to look at him, my first instinct to apologize, but it was clear he was too drunk to even recognize where he was. So I tried to step past him. His head bobbed upright and his eyes brought me into focus. "Hey you," he said. "You spilled my beer."

"No. Sorry, buddy. You bumped into me."

His eyes grew bigger and he leaned in toward me, too close. "Man, you are beautiful," he said.

"Thank you," I said trying to push by him.

"What's your hurry, little lady?"

"I'm not interested, okay. Have a good night."

"Oh, you're going to be like that. All uptight."

"Whatever you say. Now excuse me."

As I took a step to move past him, he grabbed me by the elbow.

I spun around, knocked his hand from my arm,

stomped on his foot, and gave him a little shove. Just enough to get the space I needed.

In his drunken state, that's all it took, and down he went. His friends roared with laughter as he sputtered and swore. I didn't care. I didn't have time for this. Out the door I went before anybody showed up to make sense of it all.

Just as I stepped outside I smacked into another crowd of intoxicated people. I stumbled back. "I'm sorry," I sputtered.

A young woman looked right at me, staggered back slightly, then flung her head forward and vomit spewed out of her mouth and sprayed all over the front of me. I stepped back, stunned as I felt the vomit soaking my shirt.

My throat constricted and I gagged, holding back from throwing up myself.

Seriously? That didn't just happen.

I spun around and headed straight for the ladies room, trying to keep myself from losing it. When I got there, the door was locked. Someone was inside. *Oh, you've got to be kidding!* I paced until finally the door swung open. I locked myself inside, took off my shirt, washed my face in the sink, soaked my shirt under the running water to get the big chunks off, wrung it out, and put it back on. There was nothing more I could do.

I stared at myself in the grimy mirror. *Just when you were getting cocky. Could this get any worse? You should give up and head back to Dalton.*

I stomped my foot on the floor. *Like hell I'm doing that.*

I headed back out through the bar, and as luck would have it, drunk guy cut me off.

"You again," I said. "Can't take no for an answer?"

"Why do you have to be such a bitch?"

"I don't know. I guess it's just my reaction to assholes."

He started to lift his hand to take a hold of me again. I looked him right in the eye and cut loose. "Touch me again and this time I'll break your arm."

He reared back and let me through.

Back outside, I pushed through the crowd and found a view where I could see back down the length of Bourbon Street. I still hadn't found a damn salad. Oh well. I'd lost my appetite anyway.

I called Chris. This time he answered. "Hey, I need your advice."

"Yes, you should cut that hair."

"What? No."

"Just kidding."

"Well, at least you have your sense of humor back."

"I've decided. I'm heading that way. And you better not bail on me. I'll be there in a couple of days. We are hitting Bourbon street and painting it red, Poppy girl."

"Yeah, I'm, uh, I'm on Bourbon street right now. I gotta say, I'm not a fan."

"What? It's like a perpetual party. What happened? You get in a tiff with Dalton?"

"No. Some drunk chick puked on me."

"Oh girl, that's nasty."

"Yeah. No kidding. Anyway, I need your advice. You've been here before, right?"

"Many times."

"Okay, remember Kevin from Costa Rica?"

"Wait, what? Kevin? What's going on?"

"Turns out, he's our buyer here."

"No shit?"

"No shit. And I'm trying to find him. You met him. Where do you think he'd hang out here? You must've got a vibe from him."

"A vibe? It was like ten seconds. I remember he had

hard pecs and the man could sport a swimsuit like nobody's business. Ooooh, and the Australian accent."

"But where should I look?"

"Wish I knew. He didn't seem like a cheap liquor, Bourbon Street kinda guy though. Try down on Royal Street, the higher end places. Or if he's into the music scene, head over to Frenchmen Street. The Spotted Cat Music Club maybe. House of Blues. I don't know. It's a big town. A lot of people."

"You're right. I don't know what I was thinking. This is crazy."

"Try Royal street. You never know."

"All right."

"Does this mean you're hot on the trail and you won't have time for me to visit?"

Damn. I hate when he's right. "Of course I will. Get your fanny down here."

"Are you sure, because—"

"I'm sure."

"Okay then. Good luck. I'll see you in a few days."

I disconnected and cut down Ursulines Avenue and turned on Royal Street. Royal Street had more to offer as far as diversity. There were antique shops, galleries, cafés, and street bands along the way. It was lively, like the New Orleans in the movies. A Dixieland jazz band played on the corner, the distinct sound of a clarinet the lead melody. I couldn't help myself. As I strolled down the sidewalk, I dance-stepped to the beat of the music, and dropped a five dollar bill in their bucket as I passed by.

I made sure to hit all the hotspots, any place that Kevin might hang out, but no luck. By ten-thirty, I had to admit, maybe he wasn't here anyway. And I was starving. My shirt had dried and my appetite was back. So, I stopped at a café and wine bar called SoBou. The walls were lined with glass bottles lit from behind in golden hues. I quickly scanned the room before heading to the bar where I slouched onto an empty stool and rested my elbows on the bar, a beautiful slab of marble, all shiny and reflecting multi-colors from the bar lights.

The bartender came right over. "Would you like to see the drink menu? We've got a whole list of specialty cocktails."

"No, thanks. A glass of pinot noir and a food menu would be perfect." I sat back in the chair and rubbed my eyes. Where had I gone wrong?

Someone brushed against my elbow. I opened my eyes and turned to look.

Kevin eased onto the stool next to me.

Chapter Twelve

"Ya look suproised t' see me," he said in that deep, husky voice with the adorable Australian accent.

"Yes, yes I am." Surprised was an understatement. This couldn't be a coincidence. How long had he been following me? "You're Kevin, right? From Costa Rica."

"We never got t' have that lunch."

Lunch? Lunch? What was he talking about?

"Ya came by my hotel, just t' ask me out t' lunch, then ya disappeared."

"Oh, yes," I said, relieved. "That. I'm so sorry. I got called back home and, I'm embarrassed to say, I completely forgot."

"Well, that's undastandable." His eyes searched mine, looking for me to falter.

I plowed ahead. "Whatever are you doing here in New Orleans?"

He grinned. "I'm sure ya know. We're both here for the same thing."

I raised my eyebrows and eased back in the chair. "Are we now? And what exactly is that?"

He sat back, matching my ease. "Oh, a' we playing this game?"

"I suppose we are." I took a sip of my wine, keeping my eyes locked with his over the rim of the glass.

He took his time thinking about his next comment. "I think I'd like t' order a drink." He turned toward the bartender and raised one finger to get his attention. "I'll take a Manhattan. This is goin' t' be an interesting evenin'."

He was as ruggedly handsome as I'd remembered, with that wavy hair with the curl at his neck, but there was something about him, something that didn't feel criminal. Maybe it was the accent. He just seemed like a koala bear, cute and huggable.

"So, 'twas Brittany, right?"

"You remember. I'm flattered."

"How could I forget a beauty like ya?"

"And you're so charming."

"Am I? I suppose it's an Aussie thing. For some reason, the ladies seem t' dig my accent."

"Do they?" I grinned and took another sip of my wine.

His gaze turned to my left hand where my wedding ring was curiously missing. When I had been undercover before, when I first met Kevin, playing Dalton's wife, I wore a big, fat diamond.

As I set the glass down, I made a show of looking down at my hand, then making eye contact with him. "A lot has changed since I saw you last," I said. "John and I are no longer together."

The bartender set his drink down in front of him. He picked it up and took a sip, never taking his eyes from mine. "Well then, are condolences or congratulations in order?"

"Definitely congratulations," I said with flirty eyes. He nodded and smiled and took another sip of his drink.

"So, here we are," he said.

"So, here we are."

"So..." He flashed a grin. "What brings *you* t' New Orleans?"

"I'm visiting a cousin."

He made a show of looking around the restaurant. "So, where is this cousin?"

"I needed the night off. We aren't exactly close."

"Oh, now you've got me curious. What's the story?"

"Truly, there is no story. What about you? Why are you here?"

He held my gaze for a long moment and I saw a hint of a challenge. "Business."

I leaned in close and lowered my voice. "So, what are you buying?"

"Who says I'm buying anything?"

I grinned. When he didn't respond I frowned.

"Ya wanted to play the game," he said.

I'm going to play the game, all right. I needed a tail on him the moment he left my sight. "Ah, well, in that case," I said, "are you hungry? Because I'm starving." I picked up the food menu and tossed back a swallow of wine while I scanned the options. "The Caesar salad, please," I said to the bartender. I handed Kevin the menu and drained my wine glass of the last sip. "Buy me another glass of wine," I said, setting the empty glass on the bar as I slipped from the chair. "I'm going to the ladies room. I'll be right back."

Leaving him was risky, but I needed back up. As soon as I was behind the door of the ladies room, I called Tom. I needed him and Mike to break away from babysitting the other perp and track Kevin. He was the obvious target now.

Tom answered right away and agreed to come into the city.

"I'll keep him engaged here at the restaurant as long as I can, but I need to know that when we leave, you'll be on him." Tom assured me they'd be there.

I hurried back out to the bar, half expecting Kevin to be gone, but he was still seated there, sipping his Manhattan. As I sat down on the stool next to him, the bartender slid another glass of pinot noir over to me.

"I'm glad I ran into ya, actually," he said, "before I left."

"What do you mean?" *No, no!* "The bar or are you leaving New Orleans?"

"Yes, I'll be leaving town soon. I got what I came for."

What was he saying? Had he made a connection to buy turtles from someone else? Is that the reason he told Earl to forget it? But who was it? This wasn't going to work. If he left town, I'd lose my chance to catch him. Pressuring him wasn't the strategy here, I had no leverage.

But what should I do? When in doubt, get personal. Hadn't someone said that once?

"Can I share something with you?" I blurted out. I couldn't lose him now.

He smiled and seemed genuinely intrigued. "Of course."

"I'm tired of this business. It's just exhausting, you know. I feel like I'm always on the run from here to there. I mean, when I had John, well, at least I had someone who understood." *Where am I going with this?* I didn't even know, but I had to keep him talking. "Maybe I should just get out of the business altogether. I mean, it's lucrative of course, but the stress, you know."

"Indeed. But ya don't strike me as the type of woman

who would quit. Ya're a fighter. I'm guessin' ya've just had a bad day. Am I right?"

I sighed. This wasn't the right tactic. It made me look weak. "Yeah, I suppose you're right." I picked up my glass of wine and held it in front of me. "Nothing that a little bit of wine won't help. And some good company."

This brought a smile to his face. "So, if ya don't mind me askin', where is your husband John? Is he still in the business?" He hesitated, as though he regretted asking. "What I mean is, it sounds more like the break in the relationship is what's causin' the stress. Or are ya still tryin' t' work together, even after the divorce?"

He was fishing. Had he seen Dalton down at the park? I decided to offer an explanation in case he had. "Try? When he's not stalking me."

He gave me a grin. "Oy can undastand that. If ya were mine, I'd never wanna let ya go."

I felt my cheeks blush pink.

A two-piece band started up in the far corner of the restaurant. A couple took to their feet to dance in the tiny space in front of them. Kevin gently took a hold of my hand. "Would ya like t' dance?"

"I'm not sure," I said.

"Oh, I had the impression ya enjoyed dancin'. I watched ya twirl around the dance floor in Costa Rica."

"I do, I just—" I guzzled the two swallows of wine left in my glass. No way was I leaving my drink unattended. Getting drugged by a dangerous trafficker was not my idea of a fun night out on the town. "Okay, sure, I'm ready."

We strode to the dance area and he took me in his arms. Could he smell the puke on my shirt? If he could, he showed no sign of it.

With no chitchat, just the peaceful rhythm of the music, we moved like two lovers. When the song was over, he led me back to the barstool, and when I sat down, he remained standing. "This has been most delightful. Perhaps we'll run into each other again." He lifted my hand, kissed the back of it, and was gone before I could respond.

What the hell?

As I watched him skip out the exit, I quickly pulled my phone from my handbag and texted Tom: He's on the move. Don't you dare lose him.

I held my breath until I saw the response: We've got him coming out the door.

Chapter Thirteen

I couldn't stand it. I dialed Tom. "Which way is he going?"

"Don't worry. We've got him. But I can't stay on the phone and follow him. I'm going to have to let you go."

"Fine, but alert me with anything that seems out of the ordinary or could possibly—" The phone went dead. *Fine.* At least I could finally eat the salad. Tom and Mike could handle this. They were professionals.

Right. So why did I need to remind myself to take a deep breath? This was how it had to work. If he spotted me, or Dalton, it would go south fast. They could handle it.

But I couldn't relax. I shoved in several mouthfuls of salad, quickly paid my bill, and headed for the door.

On my way back to the street car, I pondered how I'd explain the evening to Dalton. I'd found Kevin. But I actually hadn't. He'd found me. Was it a coincidence? Had he seen me on the street? But where? I had to admit, I hadn't been watching my back. I'd been so intent on finding him, I didn't think about the consequences if he saw me first.

Well, what did it matter now? We had him. Tom and

Mike were on his tail. That's what Dalton would say. Wasn't it?

I turned right and headed for the streetcar station. My phone rang. It was Tom calling. *Crap!* I clicked to answer. "Don't tell me you lost him already."

"No, we have him all right. But you're not going to believe this. We just realized he's tracking you."

"What? He's following me?"

"No doubt about it. What do you want to do?"

"Well, crap." Facepalm. I hadn't thought of that possibility. Of course he'd follow me. "I told him I was staying at a hotel in town. I guess I'd better find one. Stay on him and I'll call you back."

I took a quick left and headed toward Royal Street, to a hotel I'd seen earlier, Hotel Monteleon, an historic inn with an ornate white brick and marble façade with lions on its emblem—a very fancy, upscale place to stay. As I approached the front door, I had to step around a young woman in her early twenties who was passed out on the sidewalk. Her boyfriend nudged her with his foot, trying to get her to come around. The valet didn't take notice; it was obviously a common occurrence in New Orleans.

I pushed through the fancy glass doors and strolled straight to the check-in desk. From my handbag I produced my badge, flashed it quickly, then stashed it again. "I need to speak to your manager right away."

The young man nodded. "Of course."

I glanced around, saw the bar in the corner of the lobby, and made a decision. "Would you have him or her meet me in the Carousel Bar, please?"

"Sure thing."

I strode to the lounge and found a cozy leather chair where I had a clear view of the hotel entrance. Within moments, a tall man in his late fifties, dressed in a crisp suit approached. "How may I be of service?"

"Good evening, sir. I'm Special Agent Poppy McVie. I'm undercover and I need your assistance," I said. "I need a room and I need it to appear as though I've been here for several days. Please book it under the name Brittany Fuller. If anyone inquires, you can say I'm staying here at your hotel, I have been for several days, but, of course, your policy is to not give the room number. Okay?"

The manager nodded in agreement.

"I'm going to have some things sent over that need to be covertly placed in the room, so it's staged, if you know what I mean. Nothing to be concerned about. My suitcase. Personal items. When they're placed in my room, I'll need you to unpack them as if I've been there. You know, my toothbrush on the sink, that kind of thing."

"I think I understand, ma'am."

"I appreciate it, thank you. Expect a call for the arrangements. And could you have the bartender slip me the room card? In case someone is watching."

The manager tensed. "I hope you're not in serious danger?"

I could see the concern was more for himself. Who could blame him? I'm sure he didn't get a request like this every day. It must've seemed right out of a movie. "No. There's no reason to worry. I just need to avoid a misunderstanding that could have long reaching consequences. I truly appreciate your discretion." That seemed to calm his nerves a little. I gave him a genuine smile. "I'll order a drink and give the bartender the credit card for the room."

"Good thinking," he said. "I'll get to work on this right away."

"Thank you," I said and watched him scurry away.

Next I texted Greg to confirm my Brittany Fuller credentials were being shipped overnight.

The bartender arrived at my table asking for a drink order. I ordered a glass of tempranillo and slipped him my credit card.

It was time to call Dalton. With my eyes on the front door, I punched in the number. He answered on the third ring.

"How's it going down there?"

"Do you mean besides getting puked on?"

Silence.

"I can hear that smirk."

"And?"

"And I found him. Had a drink with him actually."

"So you found him? Wow, I admit I didn't think—"

"He, uh, he found me."

"What do mean?"

"I mean I'd given up looking. I sat down and ordered a glass of wine, and he plopped down next to me."

"Uh-huh."

"I called in Tom and Mike to tail him. But get this, as soon as I left the bar, he started following me."

"Yeah? Makes sense I guess."

"So, now I'm in a hotel bar where the manager is arranging a room for me. I need my stuff so he can stage it in the room."

"Why? You think he's going to case your room?"

"Maybe. Or get invited in."

More silence.

"I told him you and I, John and Brittany, I mean, of course, were divorced."

"Why'd you tell him that?"

"A horse of course. Of course, divorced."

"Did you take something? Were you watching your drink?"

"I'm fine. I just didn't plan that sentence. It just came out and rhymed and—never mind. It's just, none of this is going as planned. I'm having to make it up as I go along. I wasn't wearing the ring, so it seemed like the thing to do at the time. To tell him we got divorced."

"Okay."

"What? You don't think so? What's the problem?"

"I didn't say that."

"Uh-huh. Well, either way, he told me he's leaving town, that he got what he came for."

"That's not good."

"And I told him you are stalking me."

Instead of silence, I heard a slow, steady exhale. "Because…?"

"I had to explain your presence, in case he saw you, at the park."

"Right, because we're divorced. Good thinking."

I smiled. "What should we do? If he leaves town, we've lost him."

"Why aren't you still with him right now?"

"Well, I-I tried. He ditched me."

"I thought you said he sat down next to you."

"He did. And we talked and danced. But then he abruptly left."

"Abruptly?"

"Yes, abruptly. As in, I didn't see it coming."

"Hm."

"Hm what?"

"I don't know. Just hm." He thought a moment. "Did he get a phone call?"

"No."

"See someone?"

"Not that I could tell."

"Did you do something to piss him off?"

"No!"

"Mike and Tom are tailing him now?"

"Yes."

"Well, I say we keep close, see what he's up to, and decide where we can reinsert you."

"Reinsert?"

"Reconnect."

"So, you think I should get in close?"

"Isn't that what you've already done?"

"Well, yeah, I guess."

"Okay then."

The phone beeped in my ear. Another call was coming in. It was Tom. "Gotta go. Tom's beeping in." I clicked accept. "What do you know?"

"He followed you to the hotel, then hung around outside a while, watching the door. Then his phone rang. He answered, talked briefly, then left. He walked two blocks to the Sheraton. As far as we can tell, he's staying there. We've called in some local LEOs to help watch all exits, but we think he's in for the night."

"Thanks, Tom. I owe you."

"No. I owe you. That Johnny-boy is a pain in the ass. I was about to wring his scrawny neck."

"I know how you feel."

"I'll check in with you first thing in the morning."

"Sounds good." There was nothing more I could do tonight.

I got my room key from the bartender, settled my tab, and headed for my room. Dalton texted that my toothbrush was on the way.

Once I got to the room, exhaustion hit me. I crawled into the bed.

Ah, the soft sheets and comfy pillow, the AC blasting a cool breeze through the room.

And no sounds of Earl. All and all, this was a great turn of events.

I fell asleep instantly.

Chapter Fourteen

When morning came, I felt refreshed. Amazing what a good night's sleep can do. I was ready to take on the world. I stared into the mirror. *Kevin won't know what hit him.*

My bag had arrived. I quickly showered and as I was brushing my teeth, the room phone rang.

I recognized the manager's voice. "Ms. Fuller. You have a guest waiting in the lobby."

"I do?" *Hm. He's bold, I'll give him that.* "Please tell him I'll be right down."

"Will do. And can I get you anything else?"

"No. That will be all. Thank you."

Kevin certainly wasn't hiding the fact that he was keeping tabs on me. I took the elevator to the first floor and, as I stepped off, I quickly scanned the lobby. A hand shot up, making a little wave.

I smiled, surprised. It was Joe. He rose to greet me.

"What on Earth are you doing here?" I went straight for a hug.

"Eh, I thought maybe you could use a hand."

"You're supposed to be enjoying retired life, not getting back to work." He looked tired but well.

"Are you kidding? It's unbearable. I'm stalked daily by casserole ladies. They never let up. Everyone wants me to learn to play Bridge. And pickle ball, which is like tennis but way faster and somehow in slow motion at the same time. Everything's in slow motion. I'm ready to shoot myself."

"It can't be all that bad."

"It's worse. There are potlucks. Every single day." He eased back into the chair and pushed a paper bag across the tiny table toward me. "I picked up a couple of beignets. Thought you might like them."

I peeked inside at two pastries covered in powdered sugar. "One's for you though, right?"

He grinned. "Of course."

I pinched a beignet between two fingers and shook off the excess powdered sugar. "So how'd you find me?"

"Good old-fashioned detective work."

"You called Dalton?"

He shrugged. "Why make things harder than they need to be?"

"Good point."

"I got lucky. There was a late flight. And here I am." He reached into the tiny paper bag and pulled out a hand covered in powdered sugar holding a beignet, then crumpled the bag with the other hand. He took a bite. "I've been thinking that maybe I would be an asset as a consultant, something like that."

"I wish I had the authority to hire you."

"Oh, don't worry about that." He waved it off, leaving a little cloud of powdered sugar in the air. "It's not the money."

"I get it," I said with a grin. "I'm glad you're here."

He sat back, satisfied. "So, bring me up to speed."

"Last night, like we talked about, I scoured the French Quarter, then finally gave up. When I sat down to order a drink, he appeared next to me, all charming."

He sat back, wide eyed. "Just appeared? Out of nowhere?"

"I admit, I wasn't watching my back. I was concentrating on finding him."

"Makes sense. Go on."

"We talked, small talk, even danced, then he abruptly left."

"Abruptly?"

"You sound like Dalton."

He flipped up his hands in that whaddaya-gonna-do gesture, flicking more powdered sugar about.

"No call. No sign of any contact. Just abruptly left. No doubt it was designed to throw me off. But I'd already called in Tom and Mike to tail him. Luckily they got there in time to watch him leave the building. Then when I left the bar, he tailed me. So I came here. I'd told him I was staying in the French Quarter, so I had to find a hotel quickly. He hung around outside for a bit, then he went to his own hotel. I haven't received an update this morning, so I assume he's still in bed."

"Did you get anything from your interaction?"

"He told me he was leaving New Orleans, that he got what he came for."

"Hm." He thought a moment. "Yet he didn't buy from Earl?"

"Correct."

"Hm."

"Hm is right."

"What's your gut telling you is going on?"

"Well, I'm not sure—"

"Hold on. Did you say he tailed you here, then hung around outside, then left for his own hotel?"

"Yeah, that's what Tom said."

"He just left?"

"Tom said he got a call. After that he left."

Joe casually shifted in his chair and looked over his shoulder. "He handed off the tail."

"You think he'd have that kind of team here?"

"Why not? When he found you, he appeared out of nowhere, right?"

"Yeah, but…"

"Maybe you've been tailed since he saw you at the meet."

"I don't know. I guess it's possible, but… None of this makes sense."

"All right. For now, you've got Kevin covered?"

"My team plus some local agents."

"Then our job this morning is to confirm you're being followed. That will tell us a lot more than we know now, right?" He rose from the chair and held out his hand. "I say you and I take a tour of the French Quarter, my dear."

"Well, I suppose I could use some breakfast."

"It'll be our first stop."

As we stepped outside the hotel, a blast of warm air swirled around us, carrying the scents of the city—hot beignets, stale beer, and rotten fry grease. We headed to Canal Street, to the Ruby Slipper Cafe.

"Don't try to identify our tail," Joe said. "Let me do that. If we're right, they've been tasked to stay on you. So when it makes sense, I'll break away and circle back."

"Got it," I said as we entered the noisy diner, and scanned the bold red booths for an open spot.

Once we were seated and had coffee on the way, my phone rang. It was Tom.

"He's on the move, in a vehicle headed out of the city," he said.

"Do you think he's leaving town already?"

"He didn't check out of the hotel at the front desk. We have staff checking his room now, to see if he took all his belongings. We'll keep you informed."

"I don't like this," I said to Joe. "Sitting here, having coffee, doing nothing."

"You're not doing nothing. You're baiting a tail. It could be very informative."

"Yeah, well, I feel more like I'm sitting on my hands. That's all Dalton and I have been doing. I'm going stir crazy."

"You should order the buttermilk biscuits. They're the bomb."

"The bomb?"

"I read it on Yelp."

"Okay, then it must be true."

"Listen, I know you're a get-it-done-now kinda gal, but sometimes these ops can take months, even years. You gotta enjoy the ride along the way. Live a little. You should get the grits, too."

That made me smile. "I know what you're saying. But I don't like the not knowing. I have to figure out the puzzle. It gnaws at me."

"Of course it does."

The server, a young man in red sneakers with long hair tied up in a man-bun, set down two mugs of coffee and took our orders.

Once he was gone, I said, "I mean, why would he arrange for Earl to meet him, then not make contact? Then text, then back out? Then connect with me, just to abruptly leave? It doesn't make any sense."

"Ah, but it does. To him." Joe slurped his coffee.

"That's where the answer lies. With him. So you're asking the right questions. Why *would* he do those things?"

"The most logical reason he didn't show with Earl is that he saw me or Dalton."

"But?"

"But I don't think he did."

"Why do you think that?"

"I don't know. Gut feeling. I don't think he saw me until I tailed him. Before that, when he approached Earl, it was, I don't know, he acted more like he was testing him. I mean, it would have been really bold, and stupid, quite frankly, to ask him to meet in person like that. A trafficker of his caliber would be much more cautious, more elusive."

"Uh-huh."

"He'd never met Earl in person before. That according to Earl, anyway. Why now?"

"Good question."

"He's grasping at straws? But why? Maybe he lost his other sources?"

Joe shrugged.

"He's got this export business going, there's demand, but he doesn't have enough supply?"

"Sounds plausible," Joe said, holding his coffee mug to his lips.

"He's been buying a few here and there, setting up other options, then lost his main supplier." *Ah-ha!* "Maybe the guy got busted."

"Now you're getting somewhere," Joe said.

The server placed a monster platter in front of me with fluffy biscuits and fruit. I picked up a biscuit and chomped off a bite. It was the perfect fluff with that southern flavor. "Ooooh, that is the bomb."

Joe grinned. "Whad' I tell ya?"

"We need to look at recent busts involving turtles."

"Mmm hmm," Joe said while chewing.

"But that will only tell us who he used to buy from."

Joe nodded.

"He needs a new supplier. Maybe he wanted to discuss volume with Earl. Or make a deal with him, set him up as a middleman."

Joe nodded again, lifting his mug.

"Oooh, I wonder if…"

"Now you're thinking," Joe said, grinning again.

"I didn't say anything yet."

"Yes, but you thought it."

My phone rang. It was Tom. "We've followed Kevin out of town. Guess where he is now?"

"No idea."

"Earl's fish camp."

I sat upright. "Are you serious? Did you alert Dalton?"

"We did. Dalton and Earl are out on his library route. Kevin rented an airboat with a driver. As soon as he left the dock, we flashed our badges. The owner confirmed that's where he was headed. Now we wait. He assures us the driver will give us any details we want when Kevin gets back."

"And had he checked out of the hotel?"

"Not yet."

"Great. Good job. Call me when you have details?"

"Will do."

Cool air puffed out of the air conditioner. I looked down at my plate of delicious food. "Maybe you're right," I said. "Maybe I need to relax, sit right here and enjoy my breakfast. Tom and Mike can handle the swamp work."

"Atta girl." He held up his coffee mug and I clinked mine with his.

"So, what were you thinking, before the phone rang?"

I waved it off. "Nothing, it won't work."

"Tell me."

I let out a puff of breath. "Okay. He already thinks I'm a player. I was thinking maybe I could get him to buy from me. You know, he's got the export thing going, all set up, and I've been, supposedly, buying already. I could convince him I've got a good supply chain set up."

"But wouldn't he think you'd have an exporter then too? Or you were doing it yourself?"

"Right, that's the flaw in my plan."

"Okay, so you're a buyer, the exporter you were working with got busted recently. That's easy to claim. We just find a recent case, make sure the guy's in jail, we restrict his communication, and you can use it."

I was nodding my head. "That could work."

"What's the hesitation?"

"You're assuming I'll get another chance at it."

"I've got a good feeling about it."

"I don't know," I said, swirling butter in my grits. "It feels too contrived. He'll see right through it."

"You can sell it."

I shook my head. It didn't feel quite right. There had to be another way.

"While you think about it," Joe said, "I need a cigarette."

I looked up at him in surprise. "What? I didn't know you smoked."

"I don't. But it's a plausible excuse to go stand outside the door and look around."

"You're a genius."

"I've had my moments."

He got up from the booth and went to the cashier to pay the bill. When he came back, he had a cigarette and a lighter in his hand. "The cook is quite the negotiator. Only cost me ten dollars," he said with a grin. "I'll be back in five minutes."

I watched as he left through the door, paced outside the window looking around, then came back in.

"Nothing," he said. "I've got an idea though. Give me your phone."

I handed it over without hesitation.

He told me to smile and took several pictures of me. Then he handed it back. "Now take some of me. Make sure to get every angle."

I did as he said.

"We'll take more throughout the day. I assume you have someone who can sort through them."

"Sure do," I said. "Good thinking." I sent the photos to Greg.

Joe rose from the booth. "Now where would you like to go next, my dear?"

"I'm thinking a carriage ride," I said. "Then a cemetery tour. Oh, and we have to check out Magazine Street."

He took my hand. "The day is young."

Chapter Fifteen

By the end of the day, Joe and I had sent over four hundred photos to Greg to analyze. We hadn't spotted a tail on our own. He was either very good, or we didn't have one. Or the long shot possibility—we had a full surveillance detail tag team.

Tom called back with an update. Kevin had searched Earl's fish camp, but the airboat driver reported that he seemed frustrated that he didn't find what he had been looking for. He stopped for a late lunch, a fried catfish po' boy, and was headed back into the city.

"Back to the hotel?" I asked.

They didn't know. "We'll give you a play-by-play. That's the best we can do."

I turned to Joe. "I think I should be waiting in the lobby of his hotel. Why not? He popped up on me. Two can play that game. He'll be amused, or put off balance. Either way, it will work to my advantage."

"I say go for it." He paused. "What's your plan?"

I shook my head. "I have no idea."

Joe grinned. "Excellent."

"I'm thinking of it as a Hail Mary. I don't have time to find a recent bust or anything else."

"Well, I'll be standing by, back at the Hotel Monteleon. Call me if you need anything."

I gave him a big hug. "Thanks. Thanks for everything."

"What? I did nothing but stroll around the French Quarter like a tourist."

"You made all the difference."

He grinned. "I was glad to help."

The evening light streamed into the stately lobby of the Sheraton through floor-to-ceiling glass windows. In the center of the atrium, a round bar stood, adorned with beams mimicking a dome-like structure, with a brass pelican at the apex. I needed a spot to wait where I could see the main entrance, and Kevin, upon entering, would spot me right away and this seemed like the ideal spot. I grabbed an empty bar stool.

Just as I got seated, my phone beeped. Tom texted that, indeed, Kevin was parking at the Sheraton. He should be arriving within minutes.

I ordered a glass of wine and paid cash.

Here goes nothing.

Tom texted: He's entering through the front door in 3, 2, 1…

I looked up as Kevin pushed through the glass doors. He scanned the lobby and his eyes met mine. I raised my hand and gave him a little wave.

Was that a hint of a smile? As he came my way, the smile faded. I had the sense he'd rather head to his room to wash off the sweat of the swamp before talking to me, but he still made his way toward me.

"You look like you've had a long day," I said when he approached.

"Yeah, and it's time t' hit the frog and toad."

I sat back. "The what?"

"Time for me t' get goin', is that what they say here?"

"Oh," I said. "Well, I'm glad I caught you then. After last night, I got to thinking and I have a proposition. I was hoping you might hear me out."

He was still standing, making no commitment to talk.

"Just give me ten minutes. I'll buy you a drink."

He stared for a long moment. "Well, I guess i' would be rude t' turn ya down."

"Indeed," I said, pulling out the chair next to me and waving for the bartender. "A Manhattan, please."

Kevin eased into the chair. "What did ya want t' talk about?"

Um, crap. Okay, it's now or never. Out with it. "I've got an export problem."

He sat back in the chair, staring at me. "So, we're done playin' that game then?"

"Yeah," I said. "You're leaving town and I'm out of time. I feel like fate has brought us together."

He gave me a nod. "Go ahead then."

"I've invested considerable time here, establishing reliable sources, and I've got them. Had a good thing going. But I recently lost a link in my chain."

"I don't follow."

"John always said, the sweet spot is being the middleman. I always thought he was full of shit. He didn't want to get his hands dirty on either end, where the feds crack down hardest. You know what I'm saying?"

The bartender slid the Manhattan across the bar top to Kevin. We both went silent until he was out of ear shot again.

I leaned in. "I got product. A steady supply. All set up and ready to go. But John had all the connections on the other end. His exporter refuses to work with me."

Kevin was playing it cool. He slowly sipped his drink. "What's this got t' do with me?"

"Simple. You obviously got something going. I'm not stupid. For me, a cut of the profit is worth more than no profit."

"Right," he said. "But faw me, a cut in the profit is a cut in the profit. Why would I do that?"

Damn. Okay. New tactic. "You could be completely hands off. No more time in the swamp. I'll handle that side of things. You give all your attention to the other side."

"Why would I trust ya? Ya once stood me up for lunch."

I grinned. "I did. Yes. But that was a different time."

"What's different?"

I sat up straighter, taking control. "I'm making all the decisions now."

He smiled, considering my declaration. "Yeah, so why won't this other guy work with ya then?"

I shrugged. "Misogyny? The patriarchal order? He doesn't like the way I do my hair? Who knows."

Kevin turned toward the wall of windows, thought for a long time before saying, "This buildin' sure is gorgeous, isn't i'?"

"It is," I said. *What the hell is he doing?*

"I man, the architecture is astoundin'."

Architecture? I managed to mutter, "Uh-huh." *Is he stalling?*

Finally, he turned back to me. "Are ya sayin', ya can provide anythin'? That your network is such that all i have t' do is place an order?"

I nodded. Now we were getting somewhere. "I am."

He leaned in close. "Could ya get an alligator snappin' turtle?"

"Anything you want," I said, trying not to show my excitement. He was taking the bait. Alligator snapping turtles are threatened by human exploitation in all U.S. states, but especially in Louisiana, and have pending status as an endangered species. "What size do you want?"

"I got a guy's been askin' for a big boy. The bigger the better. If ya could deliver that..."

"Not only can I do it, I can do it by tomorrow." I added a cocky eyebrow, just to drive it home.

"Ya kiddin' me."

"Nope. I know you're on your way out of town. I don't want to hold you up." I paused, as if I were coming up with an offer on the fly. "I tell you what, I get the turtle, prove myself, then we talk some more. Deal?"

"Tomorrow? I'm not prepared t'—"

"C'mon, you just asked for it. I'll have it packed for shipment, ready to go."

"Tomorrow?" he asked in disbelief.

"Yeah, that's what I said. What's the problem?"

"No problem. Okay, fine." He tapped a finger on the bar. "But I'm not really sure that..." His words trailed off.

"Really sure what?"

He seemed to be pondering a decision, weighing the odds.

Finally, he said, "If I'm undastandin' ya correctly, ya tellin' me ya can supply anythin' I can order."

I nodded. Was it too much?

"Diamond-backed terrapins? Box turtle? Red-eared sliders?"

I nodded. "You name it."

"Gopher tortoises? Ringed map turtles?"

I hesitated. He was testing me. I couldn't push it. "I'd have to check on the tortoise."

He sat back. "Fair enough."

"Listen," I said. "I know I'm taking a risk, telling you this. And I hate to admit my situation. But, like I said before, I think we were meant to run into each other. Sometimes fate intervenes."

Oh geez. What was I saying? *All of a sudden I sound like I'm in a Nora Ephron movie. Too much, McVie.*

"I don't know," he said, staring at the ice in his drink as he gently swirled it around.

Shit.

"Maybe just the snapper."

That would be enough to establish a relationship. Like Joe said, this op could take months. This was a good start. "Okay. I get it. Done. Maybe I'll bring some others, just for you to take a look, prove what I'm saying. No pressure to buy. Deal?"

He shrugged. "That's fine."

"Good. Ten-thirty tomorrow morning. I'll meet you at, uh—"

"My room. Bring i' here, t' my room."

That's odd. "Sure, why not?"

"Packed in a suitcase. It's a great cover."

He gave me his room number and agreed to meet with me at ten-thirty.

"You won't regret it," I said as he rose from the chair and drained the rest of the Manhattan. "We're going to have a great partnership."

I called Dalton right away. "I got 'em. I got 'em! All I need is a huge alligator snapping turtle, packed and ready to go. And then maybe some—"

"What? Slow down."

I talked while speed walking to my hotel. "Kevin. He wants to buy an alligator snapping turtle, the bigger the better. I need it for a ten-thirty meet tomorrow."

"In the morning?"

"Yeah, I told him I could do it."

"Of course you did."

"It's a test, to see if I actually do have the resources that I told him I did."

"I understand."

"I also need any other species we can tempt him with. I told him I'd bring others to show off what I can supply. He asked about Diamond-backed terrapins and Box turtles and others. He was testing me."

"I'm sure he was."

"So we need Earl to get them."

"What? Wait."

"You need to get him on it right away."

"I can't. I'm in the city."

"What? Why?"

"Hyland said I could cut him loose. Kevin is the target of our investigation now. He fulfilled his obligation."

"But I need those turtles. We don't have time to get them through regular channels."

Dalton sighed. "Well, I'm at the hotel with Joe."

"Fine. I'll be right there."

Ten minutes later, Dalton, Joe, and I were gathered around a table in a private conference room.

"What's the strategy?" Joe asked.

"This is a first step. I give him the snapper, he takes it. I implied that I'd like to talk more about a partnership."

Dalton looked at me, eyebrows raised.

"Yes, I implied. Quite adamantly. But it felt right. He was open."

"Okay," Dalton said. "We need to tread carefully. Very carefully. He asked for the turtle as a test. No doubt there. But he might not be testing whether you can provide a turtle. He might be testing something else. Like if you're a cop."

"I know. I'm going to have to go in alone, with no wire, no backup."

"That's dangerous."

"I don't think so. Not really. I mean, I can handle myself."

"And we need to be very cautious from the beginning. We don't want him to have cause to claim entrapment."

"Entrapment?" I said. "Why would you jump to that conclusion?"

"It's not that farfetched," Joe offered.

"But I've done nothing that could be perceived as a threat or harassment."

"Don't forget," Dalton said, "Even flattery to induce a defendant to a commit crime can be considered entrapment."

"Well, when I said I was surprised he remembered my name, he said, 'How could I forget a beauty like you?' so, he's the one flattering. I say, I can flatter back all I want."

"That aside," Joe said, his eyes on Dalton. "Let's stay focused, shall we?"

Dalton pressed on. "I'm just saying, we need to play this by the book. We don't want him to get off because of some small mistake."

"I understand," I said. "By the book."

"And this might take months, maybe even years."

"You don't have to remind me."

Dalton stared. "I know patience isn't your strong suit."

I stared back. "That's correct."

That shut him up.

"Okay, what about the turtles?" I asked. "We need Earl on this."

"I talked to Tom already," Dalton said. "He's going to press Johnny for sources. I figured we needed the evening to plan, to strategize. We need to talk about how you're going to approach this thing, how to make sure—"

Joe put his hand on Dalton's arm and squeezed. "She got this far, I think she's got a good handle on things."

Dalton stared at him for a moment, then seemed to realize the wisdom in Joe's words. "You're right." He turned back to me. "You've got this."

His phone rang. I watched as Dalton nodded, grimaced, nodded again. Finally, he clicked end.

"What?" I burst.

"Johnny's a no go. Tom's convinced—and these are his words— he's a dimwit at the end of the chain. He'd have to go catch them all tonight. It's not going to happen. He doesn't have the network."

I leaped from my chair. "It's Earl then, and that son-of-bitch better come through."

Chapter Sixteen

Earl was the sleaziest perp I'd ever had to deal with. When I'd first met him, my gut screamed that he was enjoying toying with us. Now I knew he was just another sneaky weasel who'd bang some other woman in the parking lot when out on the town with his girlfriend. Deadbeats like him made my skin crawl.

By the time we got to his fish camp, the sun had gone down and the cicadas were chirping like the Vienna Boys Choir. I drew in a calming breath. I'd hoped I'd never have to set foot in this place again.

All the lights were out, but as we tied off and stepped from the fishing boat. Piddles met us, wagging his tail.

Then I heard the distinctive sounds of Earl and Sandy making up for lost time.

"I guess things with Al didn't work out," I said to Dalton.

He smirked.

We stepped inside and Dalton flipped on the light switch. Empty beer bottles were strewn about the place.

"Let me handle this, okay?" Dalton said. "Earl's not going to be too happy about it."

"Fine," I said and took a seat on the folding chair.

"Up and at 'em," Dalton hollered as he plopped onto the couch.

"What the hell?" Earl bellowed from the bedroom.

"Need you out here," Dalton said, exuding calm.

Earl shot out of the bedroom like a bull out of the chute. Made me wonder how Dalton was going to handle the next eight seconds. Earl stood buck-naked, staring at Dalton, hands on his hips. "What the hell, man?"

"We need your help," Dalton said.

"What? No way. I's done. Get da hell out. I's gettin' my papers in da mornin'." He jabbed his thumb toward the door. "So piss off."

"Yeah, about that," Dalton said, slowly rising from the couch. He tossed Earl a pillow to cover himself. "Something's come up."

"Oh no, you som-bitch. Ain't nuttin'. You said I was done, now ya jus' yankin' my damn chain, 'cause dat's what cops do."

"Believe me, I don't want to be back here anymore than you want me to. But, we've got a bit of a complication, and if you want us out of your hair for good, you've got to do this last thing."

Sandy stumbled though the doorway, the sheet wrapped around her. When she saw me, she smiled. "Well, hey dere Poppy."

"Hi Sandy. Sorry about this."

She shrugged, a resounding commentary of Earl's performance.

"Whatever it is, I ain't doin' it," Earl said. He tossed the pillow at Dalton, grabbed Sandy by the arm, tugged her back into the bedroom, and slammed the door.

Dalton shook his head.

"It's my turn then?" I said.

Dalton shrugged.

I pushed through the door, grabbed Earl by the ear, tugged him from the bed, and shoved him against the wall. "Listen up, Earl. We aren't asking. Got it? If you don't think I'll march your ass down to jail right this minute, think again."

"You can't. I got—"

"I can and I will. Remember that shooting spree you went on, back on Sandy's birthday? You shot a whooping crane, an endangered species. That's a federal crime. And I'm going to make it my personal mission to see you punished for it."

There was a flicker of fear in his eyes. He turned on Sandy. "Ya dumb bitch, yackin' ya jaws. I swear ta God, woman, you jus' don't know when ta keep yer damn mouth shut."

"Hey," I said, smacking him on the arm.

He spun on me.

"Focus. Jail. Now. Or you do this one little thing. You choose."

He knew I wasn't bluffing. He shrugged from my grip. "Fine. Bitch."

"Fine. Earl." I stared at him for a moment for good measure. "Now get some clothes on. You've got work to do." I turned my back on him and walked out.

Two minutes later he appeared in the living room clad in jeans and a ratty, stained T-shirt. He plopped down on the chair. "What?"

"I need some turtles and I need them by morning."

"Come on now. Y'all can't be serious."

I stared.

"And ya expect me to go ketch 'em? I can't—"

"Earl, cut the crap. I need you to go out to your buddies in the swamp and get what I need."

"What? So you can arrest me fer buyin' again?" He crossed his arms across his chest. "No way. I ain't dat stupid."

"I promise, you've got a get-out-of-jail-free-card on this one. You get exactly what I need, and we won't bother you again."

"Yeah, and ya said dat da last time."

I shrugged. "Yeah, whatever, life sucks, I know." I handed him the list.

He scanned it. "What makes ya think—?"

"Don't even. Just get them."

He huffed. "In the damn dark?"

"Don't tell me you're afraid of the dark."

A grimace formed on his face. "No. But da guys I gotta git dem from, dey don't take too kindly ta nighttime visits."

"Not my problem. Why don't you start with your friend Al?"

His beady eyes looked me up and down. "And ya swear dis is da end of it?"

"Unless you break some other laws."

"Pfft. Well, fine den. I'll be back in a coupla hours." He started for the door.

I blocked his way. "Oh no. We're going with you."

He shook his head. "Oh, no you ain't."

"You don't get to make that call."

He sat back down and crossed his arms. "I do. 'Cause you can't make me. You wanna drag me off ta jail, fine. Then go on ahead."

"He can go," Dalton said.

I spun on him. "What?"

"Earl can go alone."

"But—"

He shook his head. I wanted to punch him, but something in his expression made me stop. "Fine."

Earl smirked at me, got up, and disappeared through the door.

"What the hell?" I said to Dalton.

"Call him what you want, but he's got some code of ethics. He wasn't going to give up his buddies. We could fight with him, or let him get what we need to catch Kevin."

I huffed. He was right.

I went to the refrigerator for a beer.

Sandy emerged from the bedroom, a box in her hands. "Hey, y'all wanna play Yahtzee?"

Chapter Seventeen

By the time Earl finally returned, I was ready to explode with anxiety. Relying on him for this op to move forward was more than I could stomach.

"I got four outta da five. Take it or leave it," he said, facing the refrigerator as he went for a beer.

"Did you get the snapper?"

He spun around as he slammed the fridge door shut, popped the top off the bottle of Budweiser, glared at me, then in a snotty mimic, said, "Yeah, I got da damn snap-pa." He flicked his wrist, gesturing toward the door. "Now be gone wit y'all."

"Gladly."

He wagged his dirty finger at me. "Now 'member, I did ya'll dis favor."

Dalton gave me his let-it-go wink.

On the porch were two plastic bins, each with several turtles inside. The alligator snapper had its legs and snout duct-taped. I clamped my teeth together.

"Let's just load these up and get out of here," Dalton said. "We got what we need."

. . .

I arrived at the hotel at ten fifteen in the morning, ready to go. The alligator snapping turtle had been cleverly packed inside a large, leather suitcase, snugged amid packing peanuts and newspaper. I felt sorry for the hefty guy, but there was no other choice. I whispered a thank you to him and told him that after his duty, I'd make sure he got to go to a home where he'd be spoiled like the king he was.

The other turtles were all crammed into a second suitcase. I drew in a breath. *It will be okay.*

I put the heavy suitcases on a luggage cart and made my way to Kevin's room, a little more nervous than I'd anticipated. Dalton was right. This was a big deal. One wrong move, and I could lose him. It wasn't just about a transfer of a turtle; he had to believe with everything I said, and did, that I was in the turtle trafficking business, too.

As I took the elevator to the eleventh floor, I wondered how much air the turtle might need. We hadn't poked holes in the suitcase. But I had to trust that the fisheries and wildlife guys Joe had called knew what they were doing.

When the elevator doors opened, I drew in a deep breath to calm myself before I wheeled the cart down the hall to room 1186. I knocked on the door and, within moments, it swung open. Kevin was standing there grinning.

Part of me was surprised to see him. I'd worried all night that he'd bail or he'd already be gone. Things were going so well, I was starting to lose trust in my judgment.

"Good mornin'," he said. "I see ya do what ya say you're goin' t'. I have t' admit, I wasn't sure if ya'd show up."

"Well, here I am. And I think you're gonna love this guy." I pushed the luggage cart right into his room. I didn't think lingering in the hall was a good idea, and I didn't want him to change his mind.

When I had the cart all the way inside and the door shut behind me, I pulled the suitcase from the cart, set it down on the floor, unzipped the top, and flipped it open. "There he is. What do you think?"

We both stared at the creature. It looked prehistoric, with the three high dorsal ridges on the carapace, its spiky neck, and the toothed beak that could bite through a broom handle.

"She's a beauty," he said. "How much does she weigh?"

"He," I said. I'd been studying all night. Males and females can be differentiated by the position of the cloaca, the opening for the digestive, reproductive, and urinary tracts. The base of the tail of the male is also thicker as compared to females because of the hidden reproductive organs. "And he's over 65 pounds. I could get a bigger one, but not on this short of notice. So, in the future, I'll need a couple more days."

He gave me a little nod, giving me hope that there would be a future.

"Coffee?" He gestured toward a room service cart in the corner of the room.

"Um, sure."

"So, we didn't talk money," he said as he poured a cup. "I suppose that makes me a bad businessman."

"I'll accept that I dazzled you with my beauty and you got flustered as an excuse," I said, taking the coffee from him.

He grinned. "Yes, that was exactly it."

"How about if we say this one's on me? A gift," I said,

then took a sip of coffee. I looked into the cup. "What is it about New Orleans and this chicory coffee?"

"Ya don't like it?"

"It's awful."

He grinned again. "I love that ya are so unabashedly honest."

"Am I?"

He nodded. "Indeed."

"I'm glad you think so. Honesty is important in any relationship. Especially a partnership."

"Ah, yes," he said. "I know ya wanted t' have a conversation about that." He glanced at his watch. "But I don't have the time right now. We'll have to save that for another day. But I can't just take this turtle withou' payin' for it. That wouldn't be right. So what is the goin' rate?"

Oh shit. I had no idea. *How could I forget to check that?* "For you?"

"Now ya sayin' ya goin' t' give me a deal?"

"Well, I did say it was a gift."

"No." He shook his head. "I insist. Name ya price."

For a moment, it crossed my mind that I should ask for some crazy amount of money, just to see how much cash he had brought. But I needed to stall. "You haven't seen the others yet." I opened the second suitcase to show off the other turtles.

"Nice," he said. "But ya should know, I never doubted ya."

That made me grin. And I remembered a conversation that had been in the transcript of Earl's arraignment. "How about $500?" I said.

Kevin rocked back on his heels, looked me over, and said, "Ya weren't kiddin'. That's a steal." He pulled his wallet from his back pocket and peeled out five $100 bills.

He handed them over to me. I folded them in half and stuffed them into my back pocket.

"It's a done deal then," Kevin said. "It's been nice doin' business with ya."

Something in his expression changed. The door from the adjoining room swung wide open and five uniformed officers swarmed into the room, their weapons drawn. "Get down on the floor! Down on the floor!"

What the hell? I threw my hands in the air and dropped to my knees. "This is a mistake," I said.

"We've heard that before."

"No, really. I'm a federal agent. I'm with fish and wildlife."

"Sure you are," one officer said to me, his words laced with sarcasm. "And I'm a movie star. This is my side gig."

A second officer said, "You can give us all the details down at the precinct."

Chapter Eighteen

The room was small, maybe ten by ten, with a one-way mirror along one wall. I sat on the chair with my hands cuffed to a bar on the table and stared at my angry reflection in the mirror.

How did I not see this coming? Kevin was a cop. A cop! But with what agency? What branch? How did Hyland not know he was here, working the same case?

What a colossal screw up.

"This is wasting our time," I said to the mirror. Someone was back there watching, listening. "I'm Special Agent Poppy McVie, on special assignment. My boss is Ben…" *Oh crap.* I couldn't have them calling her. I had to get my head on straight before I brought this to her.

The door opened and Kevin strolled in. He slapped a folder down on the table, then pulled out the chair across from me, and sat down.

With his eyes on me, he placed his elbows on the table and laced his fingers together. "So, Brittany—"

"Seriously?" I said with a snort. "I've told you, it's

Special Agent McVie. If you would just allow me a phone call, I can clear this up right away."

His expression didn't change. "We're going to have a little chat first."

"Okay, *Kevin*." I started to cross my arms but my wrists came to a stop at the end of the chain. "By the way, is your name really Kevin? And what happened to your accent?"

"I'll ask the questions," he said.

I sat back. "Sure, I get it." Nope. I leaned forward. "But just so you know, this is going to get really embarrassing." *For you and me both.*

He frowned.

"Doesn't it seem odd to you, that you were in Costa Rica at the same time as me? Working the same case? I mean, what are the odds? That's how this whole debacle here in New Orleans has happened. Our agencies weren't talking. No wonder we're in the middle of this ridiculous situation now."

"Oh, I have questions about your involvement in Costa Rica as well. We'll get to that."

"Uh-huh." Wow, he was determined. "Can I give you a little tidbit of advice?"

His irritated expression returned.

"What if I'm telling the truth, which I am by the way, and you keep this up? You'll have egg on your face. Don't you think it would be worth that one phone call? You know, clear things up right away."

He smirked. "Thank you, but I'm willing to take that risk."

"Well, you're determined, I'll give you that. Like a dog with a bone." I sat back. I looked toward the mirror. "Please make sure the turtles are cared for." I turned back to him. "I won't forgive you if something happens to them."

"You should be more worried about yourself right now."

It was my turn to smirk. "Sure, I'll play along. But at least tell me who's arrested me. I have a right to know."

"New Orleans PD arrested you."

"Right," I said. "So how do you fit in, *Kevin*?"

He pondered my question, barely hiding his annoyance. Clearly he wanted to steer the conversation. "I'm an agent with the WCEA. We—"

"Ah, that explains it," I said, pushing forward again. "The Wildlife Crime Enforcement Alliance." They were a NGO funded by the world's elite. "You're not actually law enforcement."

"My *job* is to identify high-level trafficking suspects through intelligence analysis, then share that intelligence with governments, to enable more effective enforcement against global wildlife trafficking."

"Well, I wouldn't call arresting a Special Agent with the U.S. Fish and Wildlife service, and one on the President's Animal Task Force, an *effective* enforcement, would you?"

He stared. I was pushing his buttons. *Good.*

"Not to mention, I brought you a couple turtles. That's not worth blowing your cover and hauling me in no matter what you think I've been up to."

"Well, that's what I'm here to talk to you about. You see, you have some thinking to do. Because I really don't want to put you in jail, even for one night. As much as you've tried to convince me that you're a player, I think you're really just a small fish."

I frowned. That hurt. He hadn't believed my cover.

"What I want, is John. You and I are going to make a deal, and you're going to give him to me. Then we'll go easy on you."

I threw my head back and laughed. This couldn't be

happening. "John? You want John? You mean Special Agent Dalton? Sure, hand me my phone and I'll have him here in fifteen minutes. No problem."

Kevin looked at me skeptically.

There was a knock at the door.

"Not now," Kevin yelled.

An officer poked his head in. "Um. You said to let you know if her phone rings." He held up my cell phone as it vibrated in his hand.

Kevin looked at me, then back to the man at the door. "Fine. Set it on the table."

The officer did as he asked, then retreated from the room.

I glanced at the screen. It was Greg calling. "Great," I said. "My tech support."

"I'm going to answer it and put it on speaker," Kevin said. "Be aware, my team is tracing the call. If you do or say anything to tip off a criminal, I'll take you straight to your cell."

"Right on," I said to Kevin with a wink as he clicked to connect the call.

"Yo," I said by way of answer.

"Yo to you," Greg said. "I figured out your latest puzzle."

"Oh yeah?"

"Why does it sound like you're in a shower stall?"

"I've got you on speaker."

"Why?"

"I can't hold up the phone because I'm handcuffed to a table in a detention room."

Kevin frowned and started to rise from his chair.

"Oh. Right," Greg said. "Yeah, okay, I admit, I don't get that reference. Was it from the Brady Bunch or something?"

I winked at Kevin. He sat back down.

"What's the puzzle?" I asked.

"The pictures. The ones you and Joe took. I ran them through face recognition software and identified two men that were most likely tailing you."

"Yeah?"

"Then I ran them through our database and you'll never guess who they are."

I gave Kevin a grin. "Let me take a stab at it. Ummmm, do they work for the Wildlife Crime Enforcement Alliance?"

A pause. "You know? What, was this some kind of test or something? Because I don't have time for this."

"Chill. I just figured it out myself. Could you do me a favor, though, and call Hyland right now. Ask her to call the head of the WCEA and tell him or her to get me the hell out of these handcuffs."

Another pause. "So you weren't kidding?"

Kevin shifted in his seat.

"Right on. Dialing now." The line went dead.

I stared at Kevin. He stared back. He shifted in his seat, glanced at the phone on the table, shifted again.

"By the way, I have questions about your involvement in Costa Rica as well. I mean, maybe over coffee, after this whole debacle is behind us, we could swap stories. What do you think?"

Then his cell phone rang. He took it from his pocket, glanced at the screen, and he tensed. He answered it. "Ferris." I enjoyed watching his expression change from annoyance to embarrassment. He clicked end.

"Wow, this…" He fumbled for the keys and unlocked my cuffs. "I'm sorry. What a…"

"Yeah, no kidding," I said, rubbing my wrists.

"I just never guessed you'd be an agent. I mean, you're so…"

"I get that a lot."

He shook his head. "Wow. I don't know what to say."

I pointed at my phone, sitting on the table. "Mind if I call Special Agent Dalton then?"

He sat back. "By all means."

I punched in Dalton's number.

He answered right away. "Where are you?"

"New Orleans police station."

"What? Why? What happened?"

"Turns out, Kevin wasn't what we thought. He's undercover with the WCEA."

"How'd you figure that out?"

"Oh, it was pretty easy, actually. Became really clear at our meet when the NOPD busted through the door and handcuffed me."

His laugh rumbled through the phone.

Kevin flinched.

"Yeah, so. That happened."

Dalton sucked in air and laughed some more.

"Okay, yep. It's funny. You can stop laughing now."

That caused another round of chuckles.

I rolled my eyes at Kevin.

"You know what. Just get down here with your badge, all right?"

I thought I heard a 'yes' amid the snickers before I disconnected.

My gaze hitched on Kevin. "So, this is a fine kettle of fish."

One eyebrow raised.

"While we've been chasing each other, the real exporter is in the wind."

He nodded in grudging agreement. "Shall we move to a more comfortable room?"

I got up, rubbing my wrists. "And some coffee would be great."

"Indeed," he said. "But not the chicory."

"Oh, you know me so well."

Kevin led me to the break room where I filled a Styrofoam cup with brew, then we sat down across from each other.

"Again, I'm truly sorry. I was convinced I had my guy."

I shrugged, "Yeah, well, so was I. So, we're even."

"I mean, when I saw you tracking me after the meet, I guess I jumped to that conclusion." A reluctant grin formed on his lips. "I'm never going to live this down."

I smiled. "Me neither."

"So, where did we go wrong?"

"Maybe we shouldn't look at it that way. The fact that we're in this situation just goes to show we are both good at our jobs. We had convinced each other we were players in Costa Rica."

"I suppose," he said.

"Let's start at the beginning." I took a sip of my coffee, then told him all we knew about Earl, how Dalton and I had been babysitting him, and how, when he got the email, we staked out the meet.

"We've been doing internet surveillance on Earl and several other suspects in the region for several months," he said. "When he got the email, we figured it was our best chance to identify another suspect."

"So, you didn't send the email?"

He shook his head.

"Dammit, I knew Earl had never met him face to face. But he must've been there, at the meet. And we missed him, too busy chasing each other. I saw you and—" I slammed my fist on the table. Coffee splashed out of my cup.

"Don't beat yourself up too bad," he said. "I couldn't believe my luck when I saw you."

"So, you did see me there." *Dammit.*

"I never forget a face." He held my gaze.

Was he flirting with me? "And you gave up looking for anyone else on the scene as well?"

"Of course. I mean, I was worried at first that you'd think it was too big of a coincidence, that you'd suspect I was a cop. But after thinking it through, I couldn't see any reason that my cover wasn't still intact, so I rolled the dice. You were hard to read at the wine bar. I'll give you that."

I sat back in the chair and blew out my breath. "What a mess." I took another sip of coffee. "So, the texts to Earl? Those weren't you either." I knew the answer.

He shook his head. "We never contacted him. We intercepted the email. That's it."

"So, how did you find me when I was in the French Quarter, looking for you?"

"Oh, that." He grinned. "That was good old-fashioned detective work."

I looked at him skeptically. "You happened to see me walk by."

Nodding, he said, "Yep."

"Oh, this is so embarrassing."

He nodded some more. "Yep."

"You didn't say why you were here to begin with. Why were you doing the surveillance and why Earl and the others?"

"During a two-year investigation, my colleagues in Hong Kong identified an importer. A large percentage of his shipments came directly from this region. We've been trying to sort out the players ever since. Unfortunately, all we've got is a list of locals who probably collect, but we haven't been able to figure out the supply chain. They don't seem to use technology, and even when we've tailed a few of them, we've gotten nowhere. In fact, the email Earl received was a surprise. It was the first break we got."

The door opened to the break room and Dalton strolled in. One look at me and he started laughing again.

"Ha ha ha," I said.

He held out his hand to Kevin. "Special Agent Dalton, Fish and Wildlife."

"Kevin Ferris, Wildlife Crime Enforcement Alliance. I have to say, you did fine work in Costa Rica. You had me on quite the goose chase."

Dalton's grin faded. "Our organizations need to do a better job of communicating."

"Indeed."

We brought him up to speed on our conversation. "So, that leaves us back at the drawing board," I said. "Ugh. Back with Earl."

"Yeah, about that," Dalton said. "On my way over here, I called Hyland. Seems Earl's off the hook. The fact that we chased each other isn't his problem. He still fulfilled his end of the deal."

"You're kidding?" I said, incredulous.

"I'm not."

I collapsed with my head down on the table. "So we've got nothing."

Kevin's phone chirped in his pocket and he excused himself.

Dalton gave me that look.

I turned away. I couldn't stand it right now.

"C'mon. Let's go get some coffee."

I shook my head.

"Fine, a glass of wine. On me. It's been a long day."

I looked up at him. "It's been a long op. A long, useless op. A waste of time, and all because of me."

"You beat yourself up too much."

"Do I? What else can I say? You didn't want to pursue this. But I was hellbent on it."

"Yeah, so what else is new?"

"You don't have to rub it in."

He frowned. "I'm not. It was meant to be a compliment."

"You're nuts, you know that?"

"Nuts about you."

I stared at him. *Seriously?*

"I know you don't believe me, but I trust your judgment."

Really? I stared some more. Waited. "But…?"

He waited, as if weighing what he wanted to say.

"Oh my god, Dalton. Out with it."

"Every case I've worked with you, you've been able to…" He grimaced. "I mean, you're always passionate and emotions are…" He made that cute little shrug. "You know, all over."

I stared some more. I wasn't going to let him out of this.

"And I'm fine with it. Really. It's part of your charm." He gave me that little disarming grin.

I clenched my teeth together to keep myself from responding. "But…?"

"But this case has been different. I don't know why. It's like you let Earl get under your skin. I mean, more than usual."

I sat back.

The door opened and Kevin came back in. "I just got a

call from Jojo Laghari, a gentleman we've worked with in the past, but more importantly, an associate of Judge Landry."

I spun in my chair. "The judge in Earl's case."

"You're not going to believe this. The judge's daughter has been kidnapped."

I was out of my chair. "What? Kidnapped? Do we know who has her? Has there been a ransom demand yet?"

Kevin shook his head. "No. But get this: she was in Mexico. And guess where?" He didn't wait for my reply. "Campeche, on the coast of the Yucatan Peninsula, newly acquired territory of the Cártel del Pacífico Sur."

This was too close to home. Chris's fiancé, Doug, had tangled with the same cartel, and he'd been killed. But that was on the west coast of Mexico. "They've moved east?"

"Yes, and more to the point,"—he handed me a document—"into the region that is home to the rare Mexican box turtle." He tapped the paper. "It's on our list of species we've seen in our investigation here that has been shipped out of Louisiana to China. Customs intercepted some that were packaged *exactly the same way* as the species good ol' Earl was selling. Coincidence?"

"No way." I said, my blood pumping again. I turned to Dalton. "We've got to get down there."

Kevin continued, "I can have my assistant book a flight for the three of us right now."

Dalton shook his head, his eyes locked with mine. "If that's true, Earl's still in play."

I took a step back. "Oh no. No. I can't take another minute with Earl. I can't."

He shook his head, looked to Kevin for a long moment, then back to me, his expression pained. "Don't worry. I'll do it. Just... just be careful down there."

. . .

Dalton paced.

"C'mon. Sit down with me," I said. "We only have one hour before I have to get on that plane."

"I know," he said, his gaze toward the window, as though he purposefully wouldn't look my way.

"You're worried about me."

He stopped, looked right into my eyes. "No. Nope."

"Then what is it?"

"Okay, yeah, I guess I'm worried. But it's not that you… I mean, I know you're completely…"

"Oh my god, what is it lately? Just spit it out."

He grimaced, then still hesitated, choosing his words. "Remember how Kevin searched Earl's place? With no warrant. No cause. His organization, they push the boundaries of the law."

"Yeah?"

He stared.

I shook my head.

"Poppy, you need to be very careful."

"Why can you never trust me?"

His cheeks flushed red. "This isn't about trust! Jesus! What is it with you? You're obsessed." He flung his head back, spun around, ran his hands through his hair, drew in a deep breath, then turned back to face me. "Will we ever be able to get past that? I'm talking about how hard you've worked, your career. There's a reason we didn't know the WCEA was here."

"Yeah, Hyland is so arrogant, she—"

"No." He paused. "It's because they didn't tell us they were here."

It was my turn to stare.

"They're an NGO. *Non*-governmental organization."

"I know what NGO means."

"They fly under the radar. They don't follow the same code. The same rules."

"We have the same goals."

"Do we?"

"They're after the exporter."

"Okay. Then what?"

I stared. "What do you mean, then what?"

His eyes rolled upward and he stared at the ceiling.

"Is this about my dad?"

Dalton snapped to attention. His expression changed to one I didn't recognize. "Are you seriously asking me that?"

My jaw hardened, my teeth clamping down onto one another. I stared back at him. "You told me my father died working undercover for an NGO."

He shook his head. "Unbelievable."

"I know, it seemed far-fetched to me, too."

"I mean you!"

He was getting agitated, which was unlike him. Dalton was usually the calm one.

"Listen, I know we've got some stuff to talk about. I've been trying to get you to talk about it for weeks. But right now, I've got a plane to catch. So maybe we can just set that aside and, you know, get over here and give me a kiss."

As though he hadn't heard me, he went to the window, stared out for a long moment, then turned back to me. "Can we just agree that going to Mexico is dangerous, for many reasons, and that I love you, and I think that gives me a right to be a little worried?"

"I could agree to that, if I knew that was all that was bothering you."

He got that look on his face. That impatient, try-not-to-strangle-her look. "I just know that you tend to push the boundaries, and when it's you and me—"

"You're worried I'm going to go off all half-cocked, and you won't be there to rein me in?"

He raised his hands and placed them gently on my shoulders, looking into my eyes. I could tell he was controlling his breathing. "What I'm saying is, this isn't an investigation. It's an active kidnapping-for-ransom situation. You and I know all too well how dangerous that is. Not to mention the stakes."

"I do."

"And you're not on vacation this time. You're going in an official capacity. Hyland has sanctioned it."

"I know."

"And we know absolutely nothing about Kevin."

"Oh, I see," I said, a smile sneaking up on me. "You're jealous." I glanced at the clock. "You know I have to get going."

Dalton steadily drew in a breath, then exhaled. "Oh, Poppy."

"Well, don't Oh-Poppy me. I'm not sure you—"

"Not sure I what? Know how dangerous this cartel is? Know that the odds of finding this girl are a million-to-one? Know that walking into that hornet's nest is more than crazy on a good day, but with someone you know nothing about? Like whether he will have your back? We don't even know if his intel is accurate. We have no idea how it was obtained.

"Does he have any kind of plan? Or is he just flying by the seat of his pants? Because you know this thing you and I have, this yin yang, give and take, you watch my back, I'll watch yours, you color outside the lines, I don't know what I do, thing… it works because we care about each other. Not just to stay alive out there, but what we believe in. At the end of the day. You know, things like justice. Due process."

I stared at him for a long time. "Where is all this coming from?"

He turned away, let out a little huff. Then he turned back. "Nowhere. You're right. I'm just worrying, I guess." He leaned in and kissed me. Wrapping his arms around my waist and up my back, he pulled me tighter against him, and my insides flushed with heat.

"Mmmm."

Then his warm breath on my neck and then my ear. He whispered, "I. Love. You."

I pulled back to look at him.

"I love you," he repeated. "If you're not ready to say it to me, I'm okay with that. But I want you to know."

I stared.

"Before you go."

My mouth dropped open. But no words came out.

Chapter Nineteen

Kevin and I settled into our seats. I barely had my seatbelt buckled when he handed me an iPad.

"These are known players in the area. Any one of them could be involved."

Okay. Direct and to the point. I couldn't think about Dalton right now, and all he said, and the other thing he said, and, yeah, I couldn't think about that right now.

I scrolled through the list, taking note of the names and faces. Then I switched to the internet and did some research of my own.

Campeche was a beautiful little beachside village. Not the typical spot for a random kidnapping. Taking Harper Landry was a targeted attack, specifically to blackmail a judge. Earl's judge.

But he was a two-bit dealer. Why would a cartel care enough about him to go to these lengths?

True, the dollars made selling turtles for the Asian pet market are staggering. So, maybe a connection through Louisiana, with their lax laws, did make sense. But the fact that the judge's daughter happened to be vacationing in that part of the world, now, seemed much too convenient.

Could it be that it didn't matter that she was this judge's daughter, just *some* judge's daughter?

Something wasn't adding up.

But it was the only lead we had.

My phone vibrated. A text from Chris: I'm catching a flight in the morning. See you in NOLA!!

"Oh crap!"

Kevin glanced at me. "Everything all right?"

"Yes. No. I mean, crap. Remember the guy who I brought to your hotel in Costa Rica, my friend Chris, who I introduced you to?"

"When you asked me to lunch, then stood me up?"

I cringed. "You're never gonna let me forget that are you? But yeah, that guy."

"Yeah, tall, thin, cocky."

"Yeah, the cocky was an act. Well, maybe not. Anyway, he actually is my best friend. And he's on his was to New Orleans to spend some time with me. I was supposed to take a few days off."

"Ah," he said, nodding. "And here we are, jetting off to Mexico. That would put a crimp in your plans. I'm sure he'll understand though, considering the circumstances."

"Except I can't tell him I'm going to Mexico. And especially because of a kidnapping."

Kevin showed genuine concern. "Why not?"

I explained how Chris had fallen in love with Doug and how Doug had partnered with the cartel to kidnap me for ransom. I left out a few parts that he didn't need to know, but gave him the gist.

"Wow, I have so many questions right now."

"The problem is, I have no idea how long we will be in Mexico."

I texted back: Sounds great! I might need an extra day, though.

His reply: Don't even think of standing me up.

Never!

Why did this happen every time?

Judge Landry's associate met us on the dock.

"Jojo Laghari," he said, his hand extended. "Thank you so much for coming. I've just arrived myself. I have a taxi boat waiting if you're ready." As we walked down the dock, Jojo filled us in on what little he knew. "Apparently she was snatched right off a yacht set at anchor. We don't know much else. There have been no demands yet. The judge has directed me to handle this delicately. His wife is here, on the boat. I understand she's been cooperating with the local police, but I think we all know we need to approach that with caution."

We boarded the taxi boat and headed into the mooring field, and straight for the yacht from which Harper Landry had been kidnapped, the *MollySue*.

The taxi pulled up along the swim platform and we stepped aboard. I looked directly at the woman who stood there to greet us. It couldn't be. Jesse McDermitt's blond friend—*what was her name?*—who I'd met in The Bahamas. If she wasn't, she was the spitting image of her.

Jesse and some of his colleagues with Armstrong research had turned out to be old military buddies of Dalton's. They'd helped us with a case involving dolphins in The Bahamas. Jesse had gone above and beyond, had been a friend to me. But this woman, I wasn't so sure about.

"Ah," Jojo said, opening his arms in a big gesture of hello, smiling broadly at her. "We meet again."

The woman stepped toward him, thrusting her hand forward. "Jojo, right? How is your friend, The Buddha?"

The voice fit. She was definitely the same woman.

"Yes, Jojo Laghari," he replied, shaking her hand. "The Buddha is serene, as usual. I'll tell him you asked. But much more pressing, I represent the Landrys' interests, and that is why I am here."

He turned to acknowledge us. "And this is Poppy McVie, an agent with Fish and Wildlife."

The woman nodded, acknowledging me, but said nothing of our former meeting. That was fine with me. Jesse worked in a clandestine world, and I respected that. Our former meeting wasn't relevant. Nobody needed to know. But what was her connection here?

"And Kevin Ferris," Jojo continued, "who is with a, uh… an independent investigative service."

She stepped forward and shook both our hands. "Charity Styles, Homeland Security."

Homeland Security?

She gestured toward another gentleman who'd come up behind her. "Paul Bender, forensic psychologist with Armstrong Research and former Secret Service agent."

Secret Service *and* Armstrong? I had no idea Jesse had been so connected. This was some serious fire power, and to show up this quickly for a kidnapping, even for a federal judge, didn't seem normal.

"Woowee," Kevin said, his hands landing on his hips theatrically. "Aren't we in some fine company. This is getting more and more interesting by the minute." He turned to Jojo. "Did you know there was already a team in place?"

Jojo shook his head.

"Well, I suppose a debrief is in order right away."

"Indeed," Charity said. Her gaze moved to meet mine and I felt a distinct distrust. "Let's start with why Fish and Wildlife is involved in a kidnapping."

"I think we should start with why DHS would be involved," Kevin said. "Yeah, Judge Landry's a federal judge, but presides over a small district court."

I'm glad he said it.

Jojo, with his warm, welcoming demeanor, held his hands out, smiling. "I am sure both will be interesting stories." He gestured toward the cockpit table, shaded by the overhanging rear part of the flybridge. "Shall we get out of the hot sun?"

We all moved to the cockpit, where it was noticeably cooler. Paul and I slid around the bench seat while Kevin and Charity sat next to us at either end of the U-shaped dinette. Jojo took the remaining deck chair and smiled at Charity.

Grudgingly, she turned to Kevin. "Friend of Suzette's," she said. "I just happened to see the kidnapping go down from my own boat. The one at the end." She pointed to the far end of the anchorage, and as I turned to look, she added, "Besides being an agent for DHS, I'm also a contractor for Armstrong Research."

Hm. That's quite a coincidence. This just keeps getting more interesting.

"I contacted Kevin," Jojo began. "On Judge Landry's behalf, of course, as soon as he informed me of the ongoing investigation. I figured there must be some connection. It's all too much of a coincidence. Well, I'll let Kevin fill you in."

Kevin looked around at the group as he inched forward in his seat. "I work for WCEA–the Wildlife Crime Enforcement Alliance. We're a well-funded NGO that investigates wildlife crime, globally, in tandem with agencies like U.S. Fish and Wildlife." He gestured toward me.

In tandem, huh?

He went on. "We generally gather intel, either by electronic means or undercover work, then turn it over to the authorities when there's enough for a warrant." He turned to Charity. "I believe this is similar to Armstrong's investigative branch."

Charity nodded.

So Kevin knows about Armstrong too.

Kevin continued. "My team and I have been working on a case for over a year, trying to identify a notorious turtle exporter from the New Orleans area.

"The judge recently had a case pop up on his docket. The accused is a man by the name of Earl Hebert. Now, Earl's a two-bit criminal, recently arrested for catching and illegally selling endangered turtles. When he was booked, then released, we saw the opportunity to surveil him, see if we couldn't connect some dots. We figure he's selling to someone, right?"

Yeah, me. Ha ha. I felt my cheeks flush pink and I wanted to crawl under my seat.

"And you've connected Hebert to someone here in Mexico?" Charity asked.

Kevin shook his head. "No. We, uh. You see, Poppy and I met a few years ago, on another, completely unrelated case. At the time, neither one of us realized the other was on the same side of the law. So, when we happened across each other in New Orleans, both looking for an exporter, well, we–"

Charity grinned. "You each suspected the other?"

Ugh, kill me now. I had to jump in. "Unfortunately, our supervisors didn't seem to think communication between our agencies was important. We've been chasing each other, wasting time."

Kevin smirked. "I thought I'd bagged one helluva trophy."

My cheeks turned a darker shade of pink.

Charity glanced at Paul, who was eyeing me. He knew. He knew we'd been having too much fun to stop and think. *God, this is embarrassing.*

Kevin's demeanor turned professional again. "As soon as we realized our mistake, we regrouped and compared notes. That's when JoJo called, saying the judge's daughter had been kidnapped here in Campeche. We don't know if it's connected or not, but these cartels often traffic in wildlife as well as drugs. The money is easy, with virtually no serious fines or penalties. We thought we'd hit the ground running, see if we can connect some more dots down here and help with the situation."

"You've yet to explain the connection," Paul said, his tone analytical. "Is there something in Mr. Hebert's background that you think directly ties him to any drug cartel, or to this area?"

"Not exactly. What we do know is that over the last year, U.S. Fish and Wildlife Service and U.S. Customs and Border Protection have intercepted Mexican box turtles illegally smuggled into the States. Guess where? You see, Mexican box turtles are a rare species, only found in eastern Mexico within the states of San Luis Potosi, Tamaulipas and Veracruz. That's just west of here."

"And trucking something to the northern Yucatan," Charity offered, "to go on a boat to the U.S. mainland would drastically cut the distance the boat would have to travel. Far easier to smuggle something into a softer port like New Orleans, far from the Mexican border."

"That's not all," Kevin continued. "Customs also

retrieved some that were shipped from New Orleans to China, packaged exactly the same way as the species our pal Earl was selling. Coincidence? Maybe. We're here to find out. And, as I said, Poppy and I want to help get the judge's daughter back. Any way we can. Poppy happens to have some experience with cartel kidnapping."

Charity's cold gaze shifted to me. "What kind of experience?"

"I was kidnapped," I said, matter of factly.

Charity stared. "And?"

"Purposefully, I guess you could say. Trying to infiltrate…" All the feelings rushed in at once. "Coincidentally, they were also trafficking turtles. Long story short, we busted a cartel boss." My gaze shifted to Kevin. He wouldn't have brought me along if I'd have shared the whole story with him. He'd have known my being here could compromise the case. "That was a while ago though, and a long way from here. On the Pacific coast."

"The South Pacific Cartel has expanded east," Charity said. "Into northeast Mexico, and there have been reports of activity in some areas of the Yucatan. Logistically, it's much closer to the U.S. mainland if you're shipping by boat and crossing a land border is always more difficult. It's very possible it's the same cartel who we are dealing with here."

I nodded. "I'm not sure my experience would provide much help. My friend's fiancé had made some bad choices and brokered a deal with the cartel, then his plans went sour. I'm happy to provide details if you think it'll help, but it wasn't exactly your typical kidnapping-for-ransom situation. Though, I assume with the judge involved, that isn't what you've got here either."

"So far, we don't have much," Charity conceded, "and I have no idea if this ties into your case." She handed me a document with a hand-drawn portrait. "One of the perpetrators has a couple of distinctive tattoos. The facial features in this drawing aren't very good but the crewman who saw him thinks he got the tats right. Does that match anyone in your purview?"

I looked over the drawing, then handed the paper to Kevin. I didn't recognize the man as any of our perps.

Kevin shook his head. He didn't recognize the man either. "Tattoos like that aren't easy to hide."

"I don't think he tries to hide them," Charity replied.

A woman came out of the salon and, when she saw Jojo, ran into his arms. "Oh, thank God you're here. Have they called? Do we know anything? What's the plan? I just don't understand any of this." Obviously she was Harper's mother.

Another woman followed and more introductions and explanations were made. The second was Savannah, the woman in charge of the investigation.

Charity's phone pinged an incoming text message. She read it and looked over at Savannah. "It's DJ," she said. "He wants us to come to where he is. There's more information that we should all hear."

"It's a good central location to start from," Savannah said. "After you find out what this woman knows, you can split up and start nosing around."

"Nosing around?" Charity asked.

"It's a Southern thing," she said with a wink. "A hound dog will trot with his nose to the ground when he's looking for something."

"Come on, Paul. Let's get our noses to the ground," she said, very clearly intending to leave us out.

I quickly stepped between Charity and the stairs to her dinghy. "Mind if we tag along?"

"My dink's only big enough for two," Charity said, looking down at me.

Clearly she wasn't thrilled with me being here. Did she have a problem with my relationship with Jesse? Maybe she was his girlfriend? I was here to work this case, not wait on the yacht.

"Take the *MollySue's* tender," Savannah said, extending a float ring with a key. "The captain's given us full use of the yacht. There's another smaller tender if we need it."

"I'll drive," Paul said, taking the keys from Savannah.

Charity acquiesced, but didn't seem to like the decision much.

The five of us went down to the swim platform and Paul pulled the tender up close so everyone could get aboard. Charity waited by the line until Paul got in and started the engine, then she quickly untied the painter and stepped aboard.

Something about this group just wasn't adding up. Charity worked with Jesse, who I happened to have met on a former op. But she happened to know Jojo, who had called on Kevin. Another odd coincidence. And Charity claimed that she just happened to be nearby when the girl was kidnapped. What were the odds of that?

All these coincidences didn't mean any of them were involved with the kidnapping or the wildlife trafficking. But it meant something.

"So," I said, looking from Jojo to Charity, "you two… know each other, huh?"

Charity smiled, but not before I caught the quickest expression of annoyance. "I used the services of an associate of Jojo's, a sound healer. We call him The Buddha. Excuse me, but Paul and I have to send a report to our supervisor."

"The woman on the boat?" We'd just left there.

"No, she's just our logistics handler," Charity replied, a little too sharply. "We report to her boss."

Wow, this woman was the queen of vague.

Jojo's phone trilled in his pocket. He took it out and looked at it, then held up a finger to Charity.

"This is Judge Landry," he announced. "I must take the call."

Paul slowed the boat to reduce wind and engine noise.

Jojo answered the phone and listened for a moment, then said, "A meeting so soon?"

He listened another moment before asking the judge if he could put him on speaker. "Jean, how it happened, I do not know," Jojo explained. "But I am currently with a small army of agents from many American investigative agencies. Two of them are known personally to me. These are professionals, Jean. I am just a negotiator."

Finally, he tapped the screen, and held the phone toward the middle of the group and said, "You're on the speaker, Jean." Then he looked up at Charity. "Jean has managed to arrange a meeting for me with the kidnappers."

"Not a good idea," she said, shaking her head. "It could be a trap. Judge Landry, my name's Charity Styles, and I work for DHS. Before that, I was a Miami cop. I just happened to be nearby when your daughter was taken. Did the kidnappers provide you with proof of life?"

"Proof of… well, no."

"I apologize for my partner's directness, sir," Paul said, in a soothing tone, leaning over Charity from the raised helm. "This is Paul Bender, also with Homeland Security. Sir, you should face this very real possibility and ask for proof that your daughter is still unharmed before entering negotiations."

"I will do that," he replied. "And I will send Jojo the details of the meeting."

"Is there a reason you're not here, yourself?" Charity asked.

Damn, she's blunt.

"I have… er, cases pending."

Charity leaned closer to Jojo's phone. "Does one of those cases involve the kidnappers, sir?"

"I am not at liberty to talk about *any* case currently before the court," he replied, sounding as though he'd recited the same line a million times before. But something in the way he said it… He didn't know which case he was being blackmailed on yet.

Charity rolled her eyes and was about to say something when Jojo raised a finger and smiled.

"Jean, believe me. You can trust these people."

"I… can't take that chance, Jojo," the judge said with a heavy sigh.

There was silence. Jojo stared with frustration at his phone then frowned. "He hung up."

As we continued on toward the pier, I went over it all again in my mind, trying to connect all the dots. So much more was going on here than a kidnapping.

Chapter Twenty

A man named Enrique was waiting at the foot of the pier. Apparently Charity had hired him as a driver.

Without any more discussion, we piled into his dirty minivan and headed to meet someone named DJ at a cantina.

The van was quiet except for a knock in the left rear tire. Everyone on our ad-hoc team knew the clock was ticking. I decided to break the tension and said to Jojo. "Well, it goes without saying that Charity is right. And we know why you and the judge can't say anything. But this silence doesn't help you get the girl back."

Charity touched Jojo's arm. "You not saying he's being blackmailed to rule on a case doesn't mean we don't all know it."

Jojo looked back and forth between the two of us, then settled on Charity. "I have a… fiduciary responsibility to Judge Landry," he said quietly. "I cannot discuss this."

Enrique pulled to the curb in front of the restaurant and Paul was out of the front seat before the vehicle stopped, making a quick assessment of the area. Had to love traveling with a former secret service agent.

Charity got out and stood beside him, also scanning the area before the rest of us could climb out.

"There they are," Paul said, nodding toward the second table along the left side of the interior of the elongated Coco Bongo cantina.

Charity ducked her head back inside the car. "Will you wait here for us, Enrique?"

He smiled. "I am at your disposal for as long as you need me."

Charity reached inside for something then seemed to decide it wasn't needed and left it.

Paul waited by the open doorway, scanning the street, as she led the rest of us past him toward where a man, I assumed was DJ, sat with his back to the wall, turned slightly toward the entrance, but still able to see the back.

The bar had a small stage, next to what appeared to be a back door at the far end of the dining area. Only a few patrons sat at the bar. Some hit pop tune hummed out of an old jukebox.

DJ spotted us coming and rose very quickly to his feet. "Jojo? What the hell are you doin' here, man? Did you bring The Buddha?"

I glanced at Charity. That was twice now this Buddha had been mentioned. Was it a weird cover name? Some kind of secret message?

Paul brought up the rear, gave DJ a curious look, then he and Kevin pulled two tables together. We all quickly arranged the chairs and sat down.

Charity sat next to DJ, facing the open-air front and Paul sat at the opposite end, facing the back of the restaurant.

These operatives sure were alert and organized. I

glanced at Kevin and he returned my gaze, confirming he recognized it too. He and I took the chairs that were left, across from Jojo and the informant.

Jojo introduced DJ to everyone and, in a low voice, explained to him what our suspicions were and why he was there.

DJ nodded toward a dark-haired woman in a red dress who approached the table. "This here's Rosita Gonzales. She plays her guitar here and sings." DJ winked at the woman and gestured for her to sit. "And she hears things. Tell 'em about the boat, Rosita."

The woman went on to explain in broken English how she'd overheard a conversation three nights earlier, about faking a boat theft.

"What do you mean they were going to *fake* a boat theft?" Charity asked her in Spanish.

The woman replied in whispered but rapid-fire sentences, then Charity turned toward the others.

"She said that one of the men was the owner of the boat," Charity told them. "He was with a man who is known locally—a man with snake and crocodile tattoos—who was supposed to be part of the South Pacific Cartel."

"Tell them where the boat is now," DJ prodded the woman.

"On la playa… How you say? The… sand? The beach! On the beach between Los Delfines and Mandalay."

"Those are two restaurants that share a common parking area just a little way up the beach from the pier," DJ added. "They both close way before midnight and the parking lot's empty. A good place to make a transfer from the boat to a waiting vehicle."

"Do you know the name of the man who owns the boat?" Kevin asked.

"*Sí*," Rosita replied. "Is my no-good, cheating, ex-husband, Manuel."

Something behind me caught Charity's attention momentarily. I spun to see a van just as the door closed and it sped away. She didn't miss anything.

"We should go check out this boat as soon as possible," I suggested as I turned back to the group. "Before any clues that might be there are gone."

"If the police haven't already picked it up," Charity said. "If it is still there, it doesn't bode well for any police investigation."

"I must go back on stage," Rosita said to DJ. "Will you stay again?"

He smiled and leaned over to kiss her cheek. "I wish I could, honey," he replied. "You're a talented singer. But I gotta get back to work."

Charity's phone, sitting on the table by her elbow, pinged an incoming message. She opened it.

"It's Savannah," she said to Paul. "They just sent proof of life."

"What is it?" DJ asked, leaning closer.

"Still loading."

Charity dropped her phone on the table as she launched from her chair and sprinted toward the door, DJ right behind her.

I rushed to catch up. "What is it?"

"We haven't been here two hours," Kevin said, extending Charity's phone to her. "And we've already been made."

"A dirty gray van stopped right here," Charity said. "Not three minutes ago. The sliding door on the side opened for a second, and then it sped away."

Charity turned her phone so we could all see the screen. The image it displayed was from inside the van where a frightened young girl, I assumed Harper Landry, sat facing the camera. In the background, through the open doorway of Coco Bongo, the six of us sat with Rosita Gonzales, Charity staring straight at the camera.

Charity's phone beeped in her hand. She pressed the accept button and put the phone to her ear.

"The boat they used was reported stolen," Charity said without preamble. "But the woman here overheard her ex making a deal with Tattoo Man to use the ex's boat, then he'd report the theft this morning."

Charity turned and walked a few steps, I assumed to get away from the background noise of the bar.

DJ made a hand gesture and went back inside to pay for whatever he and Rosita had.

I kept my eyes on Charity, wishing I could hear the conversation.

She looked over at me and Kevin. Then her eyes went back to Rosita, the informant, before she shouted, "Get in the car."

As DJ and Paul approached, she told them, "Savvy wants you two to go check out the stolen boat. She'll text us the location where the phone that sent the picture was last reported, and I'll go there and keep an eye on it. We might get lucky."

"Don't go charging in without us," DJ said.

"No plan to," she replied. "I'll just find a spot to conduct covert surveillance of the area—see if I can spot that van. Don't waste a lot of time on the boat. Odds are it's had people crawling all over it this morning."

"We'll go with you," I said.

"Are you… armed?" Charity hesitantly asked.

"Well… no, but–"

She accepted this without judgement. "Get in," she

said, climbing into the front passenger seat. "You two are extra eyes only."

I nodded. "Understood." Kevin quickly opened the back door of the minivan for me to get in.

Paul had already hailed a taxi from a stand a block down the road and he, DJ, and Jojo got in and it drove away, back the way they'd come.

"Where are we going now?" Enrique asked, smiling.

Charity's phone pinged an incoming message. She gave Enrique an address.

"That is a few kilometers outside Campeche," he advised. "In the Boxol Hills."

"Rough terrain?" Kevin asked, leaning forward in the back seat.

"Not so much," Enrique replied. "Low hills and dirt roads."

"Do you know if there's a high hill near that address?" Charity asked, pulling a camera case from the back to the floor in front of her.

He opened a navigation app on his phone and entered the address, then moved the map around with his finger.

"Yes," he replied, showing her the phone. "There is an old lean-to on top of this hill that overlooks the little valley where that address is located. It was once used to shoot coyotes from."

"Can you get to that hill in this minivan?" Charity asked. "I mean, without being seen from anyone at that address?"

"Yes," he replied, looking up with a grave expression. "I know those hills very well."

"Take us to the coyote shack," Charity said, grinning at me and Kevin.

What? Did she think that would bother me? When we

had met before, I'd been undercover as a short-tempered eco-terrorist. Is that who she thought I was? Or was she just annoyed we were here at all? *Bad enough I get it from the men.*

Ten minutes later, during which Charity said not one word, Enrique stopped the van on a trail that was nothing more than two ruts through the surrounding scrub grass.

"The lean-to is just over there," he said, pointing ahead and to the right a little. "We must go on foot from here."

"You're not coming," Charity said. "If these people are cartel connected, they will likely be armed. You're just a driver my boss hired. Nothing more. I don't want you getting hurt."

"I can take care of myself. I have a rifle."

Charity looked back at us and Kevin nodded.

"Get your rifle," Charity said, then got out and went around the passenger side with her camera case to meet him at the back of the vehicle.

Kevin and I got out and joined them as Enrique lifted the cargo cover where the spare tire was kept. Nestled in the back, the butt of an antique rifle stuck out of a blanket it was wrapped in.

"What is it?" Charity asked.

"I do not know who made it," he replied, uncovering the weapon. "But it fires the Springfield thirty-aught-six cartridge." He pulled it out and opened the bolt. "It is very accurate. That I do know."

Kevin reached out and Enrique let him take the rifle. "You have a genuine World War Two M-1 Carbine here, Enrique."

"You know how to use that?" Charity asked.

"Sure do," Kevin replied with a grin. "My dad has two just like this."

Charity pulled a sidearm from behind her back and extended it butt first to me.

"You're going to cover us with the M-1?" I asked, palming the pistol.

"No," Charity said. "Enrique and his weapon are staying here with the car."

Charity watched as I press checked the weapon, racking the slide back just enough to see the round in the chamber, before gently releasing it. Then I dropped the magazine out and looked at the hollow point round on top.

"Only six rounds," Charity said. "But you can hide it anywhere. I use a thigh holster when I'm wearing a skirt."

I nodded my thanks. "Then what will you use?"

Charity unzipped her camera case and lifted the telephoto lens out. She felt for a release under the foam padding, clicked it, put the lens back, and lifted the tray out.

"I have my own rifle," she replied, and in seconds she unfolded and assembled her firearm.

"Impressive," I said, and meant it. By the way she handled her weapon, it was obvious she'd trained in special ops, probably a sniper even. "Desert Tech bullpup?"

Charity nodded. "It's their SRS Covert model."

"I don't suppose you have one for me?" Kevin asked, handing Enrique back his rifle.

Charity mounted the long lens on one of the digital SLR camera bodies and handed it to him. "No. You're the eyes in the back of my head. Just make sure you duck if I swing around."

She quickly checked her phone again. She made the gesture to follow, then made her way to the lookout in a crouched run as we followed. This woman was all business.

Kevin and I took off after her.

Once she found the best sight-line, she lay down fully prone in the grass and propped herself on her elbows, slowly scanning the valley through the rifle scope.

Kevin and I found our own viewpoints within sight of Charity, and waited.

And waited.

An hour later, we still hadn't seen anything move in the valley below.

Charity crawled on her elbows toward me, and Kevin quickly joined us. "I assume you both have cell phones," Charity said. We nodded. "Since we don't have coms, give me your numbers. I'm going to head down there, do a walk around."

I flipped the Diamondback around and handed it to Charity, then held out my hand for the rifle.

Charity hesitated, her gaze shifting to Kevin.

"It's okay. I get that all the time," I said, trying to sound like it didn't bother me. "But you should know, I was the top shooter in my class at FLETC. The marksmanship instructor said I was one of the top three he'd ever trained."

"The one out west?" Charity asked, handing over the rifle. Again, testing me.

"Georgia," I replied.

"No kidding?" Charity said, making no attempt to hide her surprise. "How did you cope with the smell from the paper plant?"

"Flavored lip balm," I replied with a grin.

"Any field experience?"

Geez. This woman didn't let up. "I've never killed anyone, if that's what you're asking."

"Well, let's hope you won't have to today."

She called my phone and once I'd answered, said, "Give me a slow ten-count."

Then she dropped her phone in her shirt pocket, buttoned it, and adjusted the volume through the material so she could barely hear me counting.

"Kevin, find another viewpoint and call Poppy, so we'll all be on the line."

With her DB9 in a low ready position, Charity moved quickly down the hill, using what cover she could, and sprinting where she had none. Crouching behind a rock, she listened carefully for a long moment. "Do you see anything?" she whispered over the phone, barely audible.

"Nothing," I replied.

Raising her head just enough to look over the rock, Charity made another assessment of the area before continuing down the rock and brush strewn hillside toward the house while we waited.

Her skills were impressive to watch as she made her way around the small dwelling, checking every angle as she went. When she got to the door, she said, "Clear, nobody's been in this house in a while."

She went down the steps and out into the front yard. There was no fence, just the shack and a double-rutted and overgrown trail that saw little use.

"There's nothing here," she said, looking back at the front of the house. "And it doesn't look like anyone's been anywhere near here in… wait one."

She moved cautiously out to the side of the road where it widened into three ruts, creating what would be a parking spot if it were anywhere else.

Charity looked all around cautiously, then trotted toward something on the ground. "Found a cell phone," she said, picking up something from the ground. "Or what's left of one."

"Does it work?" I asked.

Charity held the phone up in our direction, holding it by one part, wires barely connecting it to the other. "I'm thinking probably not."

Her own phone trilled an incoming call and she took it out. "Savannah's calling," she said. "I'll patch her in."

She touched the screen and held the phone to her ear. "I'm at the location where the phone was last tracked," she said. "Agent McVie and Kevin are also on this line. There's nothing here except a busted cell phone."

Hm. I went from Poppy to Agent McVie. What the hell does that mean?

"Do you remember the… uh, associate device Deuce uses to identify friends of a… person of interest?" Savannah asked, speaking vaguely. Obviously they had some electronic way to track incoming calls, or maybe phones nearby. That would be an amazing technology, if it worked. Though I'd never have the opportunity to use something like that. It would violate several laws.

"Chyrel has another hit?"

"She does," Savannah replied. "She's texting the coordinates to you and DJ. He and Paul were about to leave the beach a moment ago but the police arrived."

"That's not good," Charity muttered.

"They didn't find anything of use on the boat," Savannah said. "But they are being questioned, so it may be a while before they can join you."

"Where is this second location?" Charity asked, walking back toward the hill.

"It isn't far," Savannah replied. "Just a few miles inland from your present location."

"Send the numbers," Charity said. "We'll head that way and wait for backup."

Why did I get the feeling backup wasn't something Charity was used to having? Or wanting? And if she was willing to wait now, it spoke volumes about just how dangerous this situation was.

Chapter Twenty-One

When we emerged from the woods, we found Enrique waiting at the back of the minivan. He was alert and looking down the road we'd driven up earlier.

Behind him lay his rifle, resting inconspicuously in the cargo area, as he sat in the shade of the hatchback. He most definitely had turned out to be more than a driver. But maybe Charity had known that. She certainly wasn't sharing any information or strategy with us.

"How long will it take us to get to Hacienda El Milagro?" Charity asked him as we approached.

He pointed in the direction of the little house in the valley where she'd found the mangled phone. "It is only a couple of kilometers from here." Then he pointed in the opposite direction. "But we have to go around the valley. About fifteen minutes."

Charity gazed in that direction, as though she was considering hiking it, but then seemed to discount the idea.

"Get in," she told us, taking her rifle from me and laying it in the back of the van with Enrique's.

"We are going to the ecological park?" Enrique asked.

"I think that's where they're hiding Harper," Charity replied.

He gave her an odd look. "It is a public place."

"How public?" Kevin asked.

Enrique shrugged. "I am sure it is open now. A few tourist groups go there each day. But it is never crowded."

Charity showed Enrique a map on her phone. "Are there any other structures near there? A place where someone could hide out?"

He nodded somberly. "Your pinpoint is down the slope from the main buildings, and not a part of the park. There are some buildings there under the trees."

"Is there a fence separating it?" I asked.

"No," Enrique replied. "Young people used to go there to hang out."

We got into the van and after backing up a hundred feet or so, Enrique found a spot where he could turn around.

"Nobody goes there to hang out anymore?" I asked, looking out the side window. "An ecological park seems an odd place for a party spot."

"The park is somewhat new," Enrique replied, turning back onto the paved road and heading north.

"Is that when kids stopped hanging out there? Were they ousted by park rangers?"

He looked in the mirror at me for a second before replying. "No. Two teenagers were murdered there a year ago, and now nobody goes back."

Charity glanced back at me. Her look suggested she suspected the same as I did—an early show of force by a cartel expanding into the area. Murdering two innocent teens would send a message.

As Enrique steered the minivan at a snail's pace around curve after curve, I wondered if we were even on the right trail. Why would a cartel take over a government-owned ecological park? It was remote, an ideal location to keep a captive, but easy to get pinned in. It didn't seem like a good choice to me.

It was worth a shot, of course, since Charity seemed to have some electronic footprint there. But it could also be a waste of time. Time they couldn't waste. They had to find this girl and find her fast. These types of kidnappings rarely ended well.

"How do you want to do this?" Kevin asked Charity, interrupting Poppy's thoughts.

"Do what?"

"We can't very well just walk in brandishing rifles," he said.

I nodded emphatically. "I doubt they'll be holding her in the main building. More likely in one of the others Enrique mentioned. And besides, whoever has Harper knows who we are. We can't just walk in anyway, guns or no guns. They'd scramble."

"Do you have a suggestion?" Charity asked, obviously reluctant to.

"We pull a Doc Ford," Kevin replied. "We are who we are and we're in a place we'd be expected to be."

"And that's called a Doc Ford?" I asked, beating Charity to the question.

"From the novels," he replied, as if that explained things. "You know. He's a mild-mannered marine biologist by day, who really works for the CIA or something, investigating stuff near the water. Nobody ever suspects him because of who he is and he's where he's supposed to be."

"And you two being wildlife cops," Charity said, "means you'd probably visit this place at some point?"

He shrugged. "We're not sure they know we're cops. Poppy and I have both been undercover for years as wildlife traffickers. If they've ID'ed us as our aliases, maybe they're wondering why we're here. If we walk in there, we could cast doubt, throw them a curveball. Especially since we can talk the talk."

"Or inflame the situation," I said, turning to Charity. "Nothing personal, Charity, but a Girl Scout would make you in a heartbeat in a place like this."

"Makes better sense than what I had in mind, anyway," Charity said, looking down at her phone again.

"What was your idea?" Kevin asked.

"Just... walk right in brandishing rifles," Charity replied. "And shoot the first person who also has a gun."

Enrique looked over at Charity and nodded. "The young couple that was murdered there," he said. "The girl was my cousin. The boy, the brother of my best friend."

I could hear the fear and frustration in Enrique's voice. His people didn't like living under the cartels' boot heels, but there was little they could do about it. Dozens of Mexican drug cartels controlled vast amounts of cash which the average police department couldn't resist. Wherever they operated, the cartels owned the law from the chief to the meter maid. Those who didn't cooperate got sick and died, usually from lead poisoning. Those who did got relatively rich. The choice wasn't difficult.

"As much as I hate to admit it," Charity said, "the two of you could pull it off better than me. And if what you suspect is true about the cartel's running of illegal animals, and they do make your alias, who knows? You might make a deal and get inside to find Harper."

She waited for a straight part in the road, then showed Enrique her phone. "This looks like a bluff or cliff overlooking the park and the valley below."

"It is," he replied. "It is private property and was once a hunting preserve."

"Drop me off there," Charity said, then turned to Kevin and me. "All right. You two go in alone, do your thing, ask around, blend in, and see if you can find out anything. I want to get a bird's eye view of the park and those buildings down below it. The park officials might not even know the cartel could be using it as a safe house."

Enrique turned onto another paved road, which ran fairly straight along a ridge, and five minutes later, he slowed and pulled to the shoulder.

"Go straight away from the road here," he said, pushing a button to open the rear hatch. "You will come to the bluff in four or five hundred meters."

Charity got out, then leaned back into the car and handed her pistol to me. "Call my cell before you go in, so we can stay in contact."

"Will do," I said, taking the weapon. "Be careful."

Charity nodded, closed the door, then retrieved her rifle from the back of the van and closed the hatch.

As the van pulled back onto the road, Charity moved quickly into the woods.

In less than a mile, Enrique pulled into the lot and we got out. I dialed Charity, heard the click of her answering, but she said nothing.

"We're in the parking lot," I said, scanning the empty lot in front of the tiny adobe-style building.

"I'll be on the bluff to cover you in another couple of minutes," Charity replied, her voice distant. She must've had the phone on speaker in her pocket.

I clicked mute and shoved my phone in my pocket. She didn't need to hear our conversation right now.

"Well, she's a no nonsense kinda gal, huh?" I said, half hoping Kevin wouldn't respond.

"Yeah. Intense," he said with a wink.

A wink? What did that mean? I considered telling

Kevin I'd met Charity once before, but then hesitated. Like Dalton had said, I didn't know him very well yet. And I didn't know her at all.

"I wasn't expecting someone here from Homeland Security. The judge must have some friends in high places."

He pushed through the front door. "I'd say." He stopped and turned to me. "The phone's on mute?"

I nodded.

He seemed to consider that a moment, then continued to a desk where a young woman in a crisp uniform typed at a computer. She smiled and asked if he needed her assistance. She reminded me of myself at that age, when I had been an intern at Yellowstone National Park.

I lingered behind, scanning the room. For an ecological park, this was a tiny facility. It looked like an old domicile had been donated with the land, and staff was making due. No one else was available to interact with guests. In fact, this young lady seemed to be here alone.

Kevin asked about the park history and staff, the grounds. All seemed legit.

He turned and shrugged at me.

"I was really hoping to see some turtles," I said. "They're my favorite."

She smiled. "Oh yes, well, this area is too dry. To see any turtles you'd have better luck in the lowlands, closer to the beach areas. This land was set aside to protect habitat for the jaguar, as an extension of La Reserva de la Biósfera Calakmul. The jaguar needs large swaths of land as well as connecting corridors to roam freely. Did you know the jaguar is the largest cat in North America?"

Kevin and I shook our heads, acting the tourists.

She stood, encouraged by our interest. "After the tiger and the lion, the jaguar is the third largest cat in the entire world. They can run as fast as eighty kilometers per hour. Amazing, yes? I'm sure that's why they were worshipped by the Mayans. Balam, as they called the jaguar, represented power, ferocity, and valor. In the Mayan culture, some thought of Balam as a representation of facing one's fears or confronting an enemy."

"Fascinating." I didn't know that, but we didn't have time to linger. "Do you have any marked hiking trails?" I asked, feeling bad cutting her off. She was doing a great job.

She shook her head. "Not marked, but there are trails. You are welcome to take a walk. But I'm sorry to say, the odds of seeing a jaguar are pretty slim."

Her cordial offer to roam the grounds didn't seem to hold any warning of encountering men from the cartel. I thanked her and we headed toward the door.

As we stepped outside, Kevin pulled me into the shade. "Have you been thinking what I've been thinking?"

"That she was a great docent and I cut her off, seemingly uninterested?"

"No, well yeah, but no."

"Okay, then. If you're thinking that something is hinky about this whole situation, then yeah. I mean, how long were we here this morning, a couple hours max, before we got made at that cantina? Charity was obviously rattled by that. And she doesn't strike me as the type who gets rattled. She strikes me as the type who would do exactly as she said: show up with guns blazing. And who is Savannah? Do you get the feeling she's not usually the one in charge? I don't like being in the dark here.

"Not to mention, I'd have my ass handed to me for their tactics. *Associate device?* They're tracking cell phones."

"Typical Armstrong."

"It's illegal, of course. But useful," I admitted. "You

know how many times I've had to wait for a warrant or other go-ahead? Wait," I turned to face him. "Just how familiar are you with Armstrong?"

He shrugged. "It's a small world."

"Have you worked with them before?"

"Not really."

I reeled back. "What the hell does *not really* mean?"

"It means our paths have crossed. Kinda like with you and me."

"You thought I was a criminal."

"I know." He grinned. "So, not exactly the same."

I waited.

He offered nothing.

"We're wasting time. What if Harper is in that cabin right now? Which way did he say it was?"

I didn't wait for him to answer. I took the phone from my pocket and clicked off mute. "We struck out here," I said. "The park's about to close and the people we talked to seem oblivious to anything going on."

"You went in already?" Charity asked, irritation in her voice.

Oh well. She didn't seem like she'd take orders from me either. "I have an idea," I said, ignoring her question. "Kevin and I could go for a hike in that direction, a couple of lovers looking for an abandoned shack for a little roll in the hay."

There was a long pause. "Let me get Savvy on the line," Charity said. "See how far out DJ and Paul are."

"Fair enough," I said. "We don't mind being part of the team, but could you clear up a little confusion here? Who's in charge of this op? You or Savannah?"

"Savannah."

"Well, if you don't mind me saying, you two seem to have an unorthodox relationship," I said. "None of my business, but as things heat up, we want to know there's not a problem between you and your boss."

"She's not my boss," Charity said. "She's a friend, and we just happened to both be near here when the kidnapping took place. She's been assigned lead."

"But you're friends and–"

"She's Jesse McDermitt's wife."

"Jesse's wife?" Well, that was… interesting. Wife?

"What's going on?" Savannah was suddenly on the phone, sounding all business. "Chyrel is telling me you separated from Kevin and Poppy."

"They're on the line with us," Charity replied. "With no coms, we're just using open calls on our cells. Where's DJ and Paul?"

"Still at the beach with the police," Savannah replied. "Have you found anything there?"

I jumped in. "Kevin and I went in and asked around. If the cartel is using the shack down in the valley, I don't think anyone with the park knows about it."

"Chyrel has the satellite close enough now that I have a good view of your location," Savannah said. "I can see Poppy and Kevin clearly."

Satellite? Kevin and I shared a questioning glance. *They have access to live satellite?*

"I'm on a low, heavily wooded bluff a little over a quarter mile to their north-northeast," Charity said. "I have the whole valley covered. We just need DJ and Paul here. We have one rifle and a handgun between the three of us. Are you still able to track the location of the associate phone?"

"It's still pinging in the same spot," Savannah replied. "Zooming in on it, I see two buildings, one large and one small."

"I only see one," Charity said.

"The larger building is to the northeast of the smaller one," Savannah advised. "It might be blocking your view."

"I really can't move laterally for a view of both," Charity said.

"The satellite's almost directly opposite," Savannah said. "Between us, we can see everything."

"I have movement on the east side of the larger building," Charity said, calm as the sniper I assumed she was.

"Someone is crossing between the two buildings," Savannah said. "The only thing I can say for sure is they're dark-skinned and walk like a man."

"It is a man," Charity said. "I saw him close enough to see facial hair. And I think the gray van is in the bigger building. I caught a glimpse inside before he closed the door."

"He disappeared into the smaller building," Savannah advised.

That had to be where they were holding Harper. We had to go. Now! "I still think my plan will work," I said. "And I'm sure I can BS my way out, if I have to."

"What plan is that?" Savannah asked.

"Well, there are several hiking trails around the park. I think we can wander into the camp, and if we're seen, we'll make like we're lost hikers. It's a good, plausible story. And all I need to get is confirmation she's there so you can send in the cavalry."

"Maybe," Savannah asked, a tinge of doubt in her voice. "But can you sell it?"

I shrugged. "It's what I do."

Kevin chimed in. "I can vouch for her. She had me snowed."

"Do you think it might be just as plausible if you went in alone?" Savannah asked. "A lone woman would be less threatening."

I looked at Kevin. He shook his head. He didn't like the idea.

"Alone?" Dalton wouldn't like it either.

"Yes. I'd rather have Kevin nearby as back up with the pistol. Charity will have you covered from the ridge. And most importantly, you'll be much less of a threat and more believable. Do you agree?"

Kevin shook his head again.

It was a logical assumption. And if they had eyes in the sky… "Agreed," I said.

"I'm opposed," Charity said. "We should wait for DJ and P–"

"Neither of them are armed," Savannah replied, a bit curtly. "That's our gray van you saw. Time is of the essence and somebody in that building was with the kidnapper when he sent the proof of life photo. Harper could very well be in there right now."

It was now or never. Charity reluctantly agreed and I headed west, around the main building, to a small arroyo, hiking toward the camp. Within minutes, the arroyo flattened out into the valley basin and I spotted the structure. If it was a barn, it wasn't built in the traditional way with an arched roof, but had just a single flat metal roof, sloped slightly toward the back. A garage of some kind. Or a tractor shed?

This wasn't exactly farm country, though. Utility buildings for whatever was here before the park?

I held the cell phone to my ear. "Okay, I'm in position."

"I can see you clearly," Charity said. "As well as the ground between you and the shacks."

"Poppy, stay cool, you've got this," Kevin said. "Give me another few minutes to move into a better position. I'm due east of you in a bunch of rocks."

The seconds ticked past.

"The satellite is giving me a clear view now," Savannah said. "I can see Kevin across the clearing from you, Poppy, no more than fifty or sixty feet from the shack."

"I'll need radio silence," I said, "but it'd be good if you guys listened in. I'll just turn down my volume, so nobody else can hear you."

I drew in a long, slow breath. *You got this.*

I stepped out of cover and started walking on an angle to pass by the shack, then turned and slowed, letting my shoulders slump forward, as if exhausted from the late afternoon heat.

"Thank God!" I said, a little too loudly. "Shelter from the sun. Please let there be water inside."

I added a little stumble.

There was no sign of anyone outside. I circled wide, approaching the main structure at an angle to draw anyone out of the smaller building, and into Charity and Kevin's line of view.

A few more steps. Someone had to be here. Savannah had seen a man on satellite.

I wanted to do a three-sixty scan, but if I was being watched, that would be too obvious. I had to stay in character.

Kaboom! A shot echoed across the canyon. I spun around to see a man topple forward. His body thudded, face first, to the ground, dust swirling around his left shoulder.

Chapter Twenty-Two

I hadn't known he was there. Not a sound. Nothing.

I could've been…

My breath caught and I gasped. There wasn't enough air.

Breathe! Breathe!

I gasped again.

A fireball exploded in my gut. Then hot shivers shot through my limbs.

Run! I needed to run. But which way?

Noise in the bushes.

Shit! More men.

I dropped down. Nowhere to run.

Something burst from the bushes. Kevin.

I exhaled.

Kevin got to me and spun, his back to me, looking for further threats.

Then Charity was there, right into position, back to back with Kevin, encircling me, weapons up, ready to shoot anything that moved.

My whole body shook, but somehow I gathered my thoughts. The threat wasn't over.

I was unarmed. I dropped down beside the dead man, checking for a weapon. Nothing. I rolled him over. There was a big, bloody hole where his heart used to be. My stomach roiled and bile bubbled at the back of my throat.

I couldn't be sick. Not now. I swallowed hard.

Breathe! Breathe!

Charity had shot him. To protect me? But why? He wasn't armed.

She just shot him. She didn't give me a chance to get in.

Who the hell were these people?

"*No dispares! Por favor, no me mates!*"

I jerked upright. Another burst of fire coursed through my veins.

Charity and Kevin both turned toward the threat.

"Come out now!" Kevin yelled back, pointing his pistol in the direction the voice had come from. "*Sal, ahora! Manos en la cabeza!*"

I rose to a crouch, unarmed, but ready.

A man came slowly from the smaller building, his hands on his head as Kevin had ordered him to do. He was older, with graying hair and deep lines carved into a weathered face.

"*No soy cartel,*" he said, stopping twenty feet away.

"That guy cartel?" Kevin asked, nodding his head sideways toward the body.

"*Sí, señor,*" he replied, then turned toward Charity with pleading eyes. "I am… *pescador.*"

Charity slowly lowered her rifle, but Kevin kept the man covered. She turned her head slowly, examining the small house and the area around it.

I took a step to scan in the other direction and nearly stepped on a weapon in the grass. It must've gotten knocked out of the man's hand when Charity shot him. The flaming shivers came again, pulsing through my body, uncontrollably.

I could've been… He WAS going to shoot me. In the back of my head.

Air. I needed air.

"Is he dead?" Savannah asked, her voice emanating from both Charity and Kevin's phones.

Charity looked down at the body.

Somehow I managed to answer, "Very dead." I looked at Charity. "Thank you."

"Are you okay?"

"Yeah," I replied, hoping she couldn't tell that I was very much not okay. I pointed to the man from the shack. "What do we do with the fisherman?"

"Savannah, are you all right?" Charity asked.

There was only silence from the phone.

Charity turned and walked straight toward the second man, her muzzle intentionally pointed at his chest. The barrel rose as she got closer, until it was under the man's chin.

"Is the girl here?" she asked him in Spanish, her voice calm, but with a menacing tone.

"*No, señora,*" he replied, his voice cracking in fear, as his whole body trembled. "The other cartel man took her away in a car. *Por favor, señora.* I only drive the van."

"The gray van?"

His eyes conveyed confusion. "*No, señora.* Is not gray. It is blue."

Charity moved toward the larger building. She swung the door open. It was empty inside, nothing but remnants of straw in the corner. A couple of shelves held several cans, some turned on their sides, all covered with spider webs.

She turned back toward me and Kevin. "Everyone inside," she ordered, motioning toward the smaller building.

"Kevin, drag that body into the bushes and hide it, then join us."

Kevin nodded, lifted the dead man's legs, and began dragging the body across the gravel.

I bent and picked up the dead man's revolver and pointed it at the fisherman. "Move," I ordered. "*Dentro de la casa.*"

We walked him toward the smaller shack.

The large hinges squeaked, a tiny scream punctuating the silence, as Charity pulled the door open and we looked inside. It was a one-room lean-to with no furniture or any sign of running water or a toilet. Two tiny windows had been boarded, closed from the inside. Scraps of fabric lay on the floor.

If anyone had been held in here, the heat must have been unbearable. And the stink. The shack smelled of piss, stale tobacco smoke, and liquor, probably rotgut tequila. It was apparent that men had spent a lot of time here recently, doing a lot of nothing.

Charity stepped back outside and took her phone from her pocket. I motioned for the fisherman to get down on his knees.

I could barely hear Charity's voice. "Can you see any sign of hostiles, Savvy?"

I saw a ball of twine in the corner and used it to bind the man's hands, trying not to shake as I did it.

There was a long pause, where Charity said nothing, then, "Where's Savvy?" She seemed alarmed. "She had to step away? Right now?"

So Savannah had been upset about Charity shooting the man. Because she disobeyed an order?

"I want a half mile perimeter watch," Charity said. "Including IR and motion sensor. Can you jam all cell phones in this area?"

I stepped back to keep my eye on the man when I realized, none of us had searched him yet. I quickly patted him down and found a phone inside his back pocket.

"Thanks. Keep this line open, as well as theirs and Poppy's and Kevin's."

Charity returned her phone to her shirt pocket and stepped back inside the shack. "Are you all right?" she asked me again.

No way was I going to admit there was still a bubble of vomit at the back of my throat. "Yeah. I've checked. No weapon on this guy. But he's got a phone." I held it out to her over his head.

"It is not mine," the fisherman said in Spanish, his head swiveling back and forth from me to her. "I was given it and mine was taken. They call me and tell me where to go."

I patted the fisherman on both shoulders, trying to steady myself and drive home that I was fine. "He's clean."

Charity glanced around at the disheveled, dirt floor interior, strewn with trash and the fabric, which I now realized was a couple of torn and stained sleeping bags.

She grinned at me. "That's debatable."

Kevin stepped through the door and came straight to me. "Are you okay?" He pointed his weapon at the man. "I've got this. Why don't you sit down. Take a breather."

What was this all about? He was acting like I was… I don't know. He was acting like Dalton.

Charity was all business. "Did you see the girl, Harper?"

The fisherman shook his head.

"When I asked before, you said she was gone, that another man took her in a car."

"Yes," he replied in English. "I, uh, *supuse*."

"He assumes," I translated. The fisherman was just doing what he was told, probably at the threat of harm to his family.

"Yeah." Charity switched to Spanish. "*Dónde está tu vehiculo*?"

"*No aqui*. This they do. Change cars. Change drivers. I do what I am told to do. I do not have… *elección*."

"No choice. I get it. The cartel is in control here?"

He nodded, then lowered his head in shame.

A woman's voice, not Savannah's, came from Charity's pocket. "Paul and DJ are approaching."

"Have their driver leave them," Charity said. "We need to camp out here and wait for this guy's ride to return. And it's probably safer if our driver, Enrique, comes down with them. He has an old rifle with him."

"Do you think anyone heard you shoot?" the woman asked. "Of course, we couldn't hear anything, watching from a satellite camera. But Savannah and I both saw it."

"I'm sure a few people did," Charity replied. "But even though the valley isn't deep, I don't think anyone hearing it could've determined the direction."

"What if someone says something to the cartel?"

"I hope they do," Charity replied. "Then they'll call, not get through, and come to investigate."

I needed a deep breath before they arrived. Maybe two.

Once Paul and DJ finally arrived, along with Enrique, Charity explained how her team would be monitoring two different satellite feeds: one through a heat filter, which would work amazingly well in the sparse landscape, as the rocks cooled once the sun went down, and another that used only magnified ambient light, and with a full moon shining down into the valley, would provide good visual.

DJ paced like a captive tiger, moving from the door to a crack between the slats on one of the windows, scanning outdoors. He was driving me nuts, so I volunteered to take the first watch for anyone coming down the two-track. Kevin quickly offered to join me.

Once we found a spot to hunker down, Kevin whispered to me, "Hey, you doing okay?"

I nodded.

"Because that was some serious stuff back there."

I nodded again.

"I mean, it's okay to admit that what happened was pretty traumatic."

I turned to face him. "What did happen?"

He seemed confused.

"I had no idea he was there until I heard the shot. Did he have his weapon at the back of my head? What? I mean, why'd she shoot?"

"Poppy, I'm not sure that's—"

"No. You're right. It was traumatic. But I think I need to sort it out. You saw it. What happened?"

He looked as though he regretted bringing it up. He gave a long sigh before saying, "Savannah spotted the man. He was creeping up on you." He paused.

"And?"

"She instructed Charity to take him out."

"That's it?" Something wasn't adding up.

He looked away. "Not exactly."

"Damn it, Kevin. I thought you wanted to help. Now you're making it worse."

He swung back to face me. "Sorry. It's just. Savannah

said he had a weapon. I didn't have a shot, because of the angle and distance. She ordered Charity to take the shot. But Charity, well, disagreed."

"She didn't want to shoot?" That didn't seem like the Charity I'd met.

"No. It wasn't that. She said if he was going to shoot, he could've already. That his body language didn't appear threatening. And that..."

"And that what?"

"That she couldn't confirm he had a weapon."

"That makes sense to me, to confirm, though I admit it was my life on the line. But that's what I signed up for. So, what are you saying, Kevin? I don't understand."

"Savannah had already confirmed a weapon."

"Yes, you said. But to confirm is standard—"

"I had also confirmed the weapon."

I turned and stared at him. "You mean..."

"He was approaching you from behind. And she just... waited."

Waited?

"Until he actually raised his weapon."

I stared.

He nodded.

So I had been a split second away from a bullet ripping through my skull. My insides caught on fire, an instantaneous combustion in my gut, and I started to shake. The bile in my stomach reached the back of my throat, and I leaned over and retched in the dirt.

"You're okay. You're okay now," Kevin said as he rubbed my back. "You're okay."

I stood back upright and wiped my mouth with the back of my hand. "I'm not okay."

"You are. It's over."

I looked down at my shaking hands, willing them to stop.

"You know, it's okay if you want to bow out now. In fact, I really think you should. Hell, even the army acknowledges PTSD now."

"Leave? No. Hell no. I'm fine. Really. I'll be fine." *As soon as my stomach gets off the merry-go-round.* "We need to find Harper."

"Poppy, I know you're a badass. I mean, you impress the hell out of me. To be honest, if you weren't shaken up right now, I'd be more worried about you. It's okay to be human, you know."

His eyes held mine, soft and kind, filled with concern. His hand still lay on my lower back. All sorts of other tingly feelings bubbled around my insides. I drew in a breath and took a step back.

"I know," I said. "It's just… I mean, I've been in these situations before. My life in danger. I've always…" *Been with Dalton.*

"No doubt. I'm not saying you weren't. It's just, it's not every day you have a man shot to death mere steps away—"

"From killing me, I know."

"And—"

"And slump over with a gaping hole in his chest?"

He nodded. "Exactly."

I took a long breath. Then another. "My mom has always wanted me to work at a non-profit. She always pushes for writer, maybe even environmental journalist. Says it would be a great way to"—I made quotes in the air with my fingers—"channel my passion."

Kevin smirked. "You've got to be kidding. Has she met you?"

"Obviously not."

"Maybe a lobbyist. That I could see," he said with a grin.

"Oh god no! In Washington? Ugh. No, this is all I've ever wanted to do. Protect animals. In the field. But I swear, I…"

He waited, giving me a moment, then very softly said, "What, Poppy? What is it?"

"Why does it have to be like this? Cartels and kidnappings. Murders and drugs, all part of it. Why any of this at all? Why is there no respect? For life, the life of other creatures that we share this planet with. They're killing animals in the thousands, every day. And for what? You finally knock off one ugly head and two more grow in its place. Human beings are just ugly. Ugly and awful and selfish and greedy. And I know what you're going to say, that most are just trying to survive, but why does it have to be that way? It wouldn't if those who have wealth and resources didn't hoard it. It's just greed. It's all greed."

Kevin stared at me. "It's been a long day."

"Yeah, well, I assume it's been a much longer day for Harper. We've gotta find her."

"And when we do, are you sure you're up for it?"

"You're right. It's over. He's dead. I'm okay."

"Good. But I also meant, are you up for working with these guys?"

"Yeah, well, they aren't exactly forthcoming." *Or concerned about the law.*

"Or clear about command."

"You mean because Charity hesitated. I mean, I would've wanted her to be sure."

He nodded, drawing his hands back to his hips. "Yeah, well."

"I'm getting what you're saying. They are all ex-military. Highly trained. Used to taking orders. So, why did she wait to shoot, then?"

"You want my honest opinion?"

I glared at him. "Um, yeah."

He frowned. "I think she's a trained sniper."

"Yeah, that one's obvious."

"Yeah, but what I'm saying is, I think she's used to working alone."

It hit me. Jesse. Armstrong. Paul had been introduced as *former* Secret Service. "She's an assassin."

"Probably CIA."

"You mean *former* CIA. If she's with Armstrong. Which she must be."

He nodded. "Typical Armstrong. Well-funded vigilantes. I mean, my organization, we bend the rules here and there. Armstrong lives in a world where they make their own rules."

A memory came into sharp focus of being launched into the sea when Jesse had nearly run me and Dalton over with his powerboat. He hadn't even slowed. And the firepower he had on board. And the way he had, without a moment's hesitation, offered to help us. He could do as he wanted. And Charity had been with him.

They make their own rules. "Are you saying you think Charity sees me, sees us, as expendable? That's why she didn't shoot right away?"

"No. Maybe."

"Maybe she just wanted to be sure of the weapon, for herself, before she killed someone."

He gave me a look that said I was naive.

"No, you're right." I exhaled. "Do you think she really wanted to give my plan a shot?"

"I think these people live on the edge."

"And she's used to working alone."

He nodded. "I'd guess she prefers it."

"Well, where does that leave us in all this?"

He shrugged. "I don't know. But if you want to stay, I've got your back."

"I do." I straightened my shoulders. "I am Balam, the jaguar."

My phone buzzed in my pocket.

"It's Savannah. We've got visual on a car at the park entrance. I want you to retreat to the structure with the others."

"Roger that," I said and hung up.

Kevin waited for the info.

"We gotta go," I said and took off jogging down the two-track.

The sun hadn't set yet, but dusk was settling in.

At the house, DJ met us outside the door with Enrique's rifle in his hands. "Someone's headed here for sure." He jerked his chin toward Kevin. "You go with Paul." Then his eyes rested on me. "Savannah wants you inside with us."

She does, does she? Fine. I gave Kevin a quick glance, a thank you. He acknowledged with a nod.

I stepped inside. The fisherman sat in the same place he'd been, his hands still bound behind his back. Charity lay asleep on the floor. "You didn't wake her?"

DJ grunted. "It doesn't usually go well."

I waited.

"I was kinda hoping you'd do it."

Eye roll. Men. "Charity," I whispered, not wanting to startle her. "Charity, wake up."

Charity sat bolt upright, shifting her butt back to the

wall she'd dozed off against. She blinked, instantly alert. "What's going on?"

"Our eyes in the sky spotted a car stop at the park entrance."

"Then it turned down our trail and parked," DJ added, looking through a narrow crack in the door.

Charity rose, picked up her rifle, and quickly crossed the shed to stand close beside DJ. "See anything yet?"

"One man," Savannah announced, her calm voice emanating from DJ's shirt pocket. "He went back up on foot and is looking at Enrique's van."

"We're in position, Savannah." Paul's voice.

"Savannah sent Paul and Kevin over to the rocks, just across from us," DJ informed her.

Charity took her own phone out of her pocket and turned the volume up slightly, before dropping it back in and buttoning the pocket.

"How'd you end up with Enrique's rifle?" she whispered.

DJ turned his head, their faces just inches apart. "I asked if he'd ever shot a man and he just up and handed it to me."

"Probably thought it matched the hardware on your leg," she chided.

"Hoo-ah," he grunted, turning back to the door.

"Airborne leads the way," she whispered back.

"The person is moving down the trail again," Savannah said. "Passing his car and still headed down the trail. Walks like a man and is wearing a hat. He doesn't appear to be armed. At least not openly."

"Only a single heat signature," Chyrel added. "Whoever it is, he's alone."

Charity ducked under DJ's arm and squirmed between him and the door to peer through the crack below him.

"Where's Paul and Kevin?" she asked.

"At two o'clock," DJ replied. "From the front of this barn that is."

Paul's voice came from the phones in an eerie unison. "To get to you" he said, "they have to walk past us."

"He's halfway down," Savannah said. "Suggest you go quiet, interpret his behavior, and act accordingly. If he even hints at being shady, take him alive for information."

"And if he doesn't want to give it up?" Charity asked.

"Make him," came Savannah's firm response. "We have to find Harper. Time's running out. Damn!"

"What's wrong?"

"That Sergeant Quintero is coming back," Savannah replied. "He is most definitely not a nice man."

"I didn't meet him," Charity said.

"Count your blessings. I'll get rid of him as quickly as I can. Y'all be careful."

"Roger that."

The seconds ticked by. After an eternity, Savannah was back and said that they should be able to put eyes on the intruder in just another minute.

Finally, Charity saw someone moving down the left rut of the trail toward them. I moved to look through another crack in the wall.

The man was advancing cautiously, quietly picking his way over loose stones. Finally, he stepped away from a large bush, halfway between Paul and Kevin's position and the shed.

The man started waving his arms over his head. "*Hola, Santiago! Soy yo Filipe*!"

"It is a cartel man," the fisherman whispered. "He is calling for the man you killed."

"Answer him," Charity said in Spanish. "Tell him

Santiago went off to look around. Tell him to come into the shed."

The fisherman grumbled his lines as if he were tired and irritated, which he was.

"*Por qué estás ahí?*" the newcomer asked, his voice sounding suspicious.

"Swarm him!" Savannah ordered. "Now!"

Without hesitation, DJ flung the door open, leading with the old carbine. He went left and Charity went right, advancing in a crouch.

"*No se mueva!*" Kevin shouted, as he and Paul came charging out of the rocks.

"*Manos arriba,*" Charity ordered, as the four surrounded the man.

He instantly raised both hands high over his head.

I got a good look at his face and recognized him right away. Suspect number five from Kevin's suspect list.

I strode straight toward him. "*Eres Felipe Pérez. Correcto?*"

Behind him, I caught a glimpse of Kevin giving a rolling motion with his hands, telling the others to roll with it.

The man's shoulders seemed to tighten and his eyes grew wide as he stared at me. "You know my name?" he asked, in accented English. "Listen, I didn't do nothin'."

"So if I check your car, I won't find any turtles?"

"My car? No." He shook his head so hard his hat fell to the ground. He made no effort to retrieve it. "I don't have no car. I walked here."

"I mean the car you left five hundred yards back."

"A green 1994 Ford F-150," Savannah's voice said from all four cell phones, surprising the man.

He shook his head again, but his shoulders slumped in defeat.

I went on. "Are you with the South Pacific Cartel now?"

"No, no, no." Pérez whined. "You got this all wrong."

"This is a known location used by the cartel. You're telling me you just happened to be hiking by, and calling out for Santiago?"

"We're just friends. I don't know what he does."

I stared deep into his dumb, lying eyes as I stepped toward him, and he seemed to shrink.

"Please don't arrest me," Filipe begged. "I've got family."

"And why should that matter to me?" I said. I'd had enough already today.

"I don't know. I just can't go to jail. Tell me what to do. I will do it. Whatever you say, *señora*."

"You can start by telling me where else these men might be. They must have other locations like this one, where you meet them."

"Um, yes. Yes. One other, nearby." He pointed to the north. "Just over that hill."

"Yes, we know about that one. You're going to have to do a little better."

"Yes, yes," Filipe said, excitedly. "There is another. It is a house just outside the city. It is about eight kilometers from here."

"I need details."

Filipe was more than willing to give up the third location, rather than go to jail.

"I've got it," Savannah said over the phone. "And what appears to be a gray cargo van is parked under some sort of carport or overhang."

"Let's move out," Charity said to the team.

I marched the man into the shed, bound his wrists, left

him with the fisherman before following the others up the hill to where Filipe had left his pickup to look inside.

"What is it?" Charity asked as I opened the passenger door.

I reached inside and took a large burlap bag out of the floor of the truck. Ripping the tie off, I opened it to show her the contents.

"Turtles." More than a dozen small box turtles were inside, flipped in all directions, their little legs slowly moving, trying to right themselves. Normally, I'd take them to a place where they'd be checked and cared for right away, but there was no time to waste. We had to get to Harper. I'd have to ask Enrique to do it in the morning.

When we reached Enrique's van, Savannah's voice came over the phone in Charity's pocket. "There's something y'all need to know."

"What is it?" Charity asked, standing by the front passenger door.

"Sergeant Quintero just left," Savannah began. "He was very adamant about our snooping around."

"How could he possibly know?" DJ asked, standing next to Charity.

"He knew about the meeting with Rosita Gonzales," Savannah replied, her voice catching a little. "She was shot and killed less than an hour ago."

Chapter Twenty-Three

We rode in silence for several minutes. DJ sat in the back, his face a mask as to what exactly he was thinking, but we all knew what he was feeling: Rosita had been killed because she'd talked to him.

She'd been there when the kidnappers snapped the proof-of-life photo. It was obviously meant to be a threat. Now she was dead.

But was it a message to other locals not to give us any information? Or was the cartel trying to send us a message? A message we'd already heard, loud and clear.

But something didn't feel right about that either. We'd all been together less than an hour when we'd gone to the bar to meet with Rosita. Someone could have been surveilling the MollySue, after the kidnapping. That made sense. The cartel had that kind of network. Or they'd been following DJ. But he seemed like the kind of guy who'd cover his tracks.

All this for the turtle smuggling aspect of their operations? It was too big of a coincidence that Pérez had shown up with a bag of turtles. But this kind of coverage, the kidnapping, everything, for a connection in Louisiana? If it was, Hyland had been right, he was the big fish we were looking for.

"It's almost midnight," Savannah said, her voice coming over everyone's phone as Enrique drove away from the park. "It's been nearly twenty-four hours."

None of us needed to be reminded. One day was about the max for a kidnapping investigation. Typically, if a hostage wasn't rescued in the first twenty-four hours, the chance of a positive resolution diminished greatly. Keeping the kidnap victim alive any longer was risky.

"How did you know that guy?" DJ asked me from the back, his tone a little accusatory.

"Before we flew down, Kevin and I went over some local suspects. When he said his name, I thought it couldn't be, but then I recognized him right away. He's a known buncher in the area."

"A buncher?" DJ asked, sitting forward from the rear seat, his shoulders cramming the gap between the two middle row seats.

"Think of him as a middle-man in turtle smuggling," I explained. "He buys from the poachers, tends to the inventory, then sells to the smuggling kingpin, who in this case, I'm guessing, was Santiago. We'll have to follow up, but I think we just got lucky."

"Lucky indeed," Paul said. "He didn't seem like he'd be a very cooperative interrogee at first, but he was definitely intimidated by your presence. Good work."

I was glad I'd impressed this crew, but I had no idea why he'd responded to me so dramatically.

"Charity would have got him talkin'," DJ said. "It might've taken a few minutes longer, but pain's a great motivator."

No doubt. And I was glad it didn't get that far. I didn't

want to witness the wrath of Charity. The thought made me shiver.

"How long till we get there?" Charity asked Enrique.

"Not long," he replied. "It is just on the outskirts of town. About ten minutes."

We rode in silence for another mile. Then Enrique looked over at Charity, as he slowed for a traffic circle.

"These men are few in numbers," he said. "But they have many guns which frighten the people, and a lot of cash that even the most pious cannot resist. They have bribed most of the police and the people are too afraid to speak. Do not expect help from anyone. Some might even join the cartel in the fight."

Charity glanced back at the others. "We go in fast and hard. Shoot anyone that isn't a scared young American college girl. If any one of us hesitates, we all die."

She got a nod from everyone in the back.

"Does that work for you, Savvy?" she asked.

"Be hyper alert when you go in," Savannah replied, her voice firm. "We don't want Harper to be hurt accidentally."

Charity had Enrique pull over several hundred feet from the target house and on the opposite side of the road.

"What do you guys see, Savvy?"

"The satellite is looking down at about twenty degrees still," Savannah replied. "The east, west, and south sides of the house are clear, and the gray van parked in the carport looks a lot like you described, Charity."

"I'm getting only three heat signatures inside the house," Chyrel said. "Looks like one large and one small person in the front room, likely to the right of the front door and against the front wall. There's a single small heat source in the back room. The van in the driveway is as cold as the ground."

That meant that whoever had arrived in the van had been there for at least an hour or two, otherwise the van's engine would still show residual heat. It also meant they'd likely be moving soon.

"DJ," Charity said, turning in her seat, "how's Patty?"

Patty? I wanted to ask, but then thought better of it. Not the time.

DJ looked up at her and grinned. "Patty three point oh," he said. "Newer and stronger foot."

Charity smiled back. "You're the designated door kicker then. Switch guns with Poppy."

DJ glanced at Enrique's M-1, which he was leaning on. "You sure?"

"I'm sure she's better with a rifle than you," Charity said. "And I know you can go through a door better than anyone else here. If you fall after breaching, a handgun will be easier for you to bring into action."

"I'll go second," Paul said. "Right behind DJ to cover any sector he doesn't."

"My rifle's shorter," Charity said to me. "Kevin and I will breach together and hopefully not trip over DJ and Paul. You'll bring up the rear and make sure nobody outside comes in."

I nodded and switched weapons with DJ. I could admit, I'd had enough excitement for one day. I just wanted them to get the girl, so we could all go home. I was happy to bring up the rear.

Charity leaned forward and looked upward through the van's windshield. "We have a bright full moon almost directly overhead." Then she studied the house for a moment. "The sidewalk from the curb is clear for a running start DJ. Any change in the heat signatures Chyrel?"

"Not even the slightest movement," Chyrel replied.

"I'm also not getting any tiny spot signatures from lights. They might be asleep."

"If they are," Savannah said, "and we can take them by total surprise, we'll take them alive."

Charity said, "When it comes to the life of an innocent young woman and the life of a cartel turd fondler–"

"I know, Charity," Savannah said, her voice calm. "And I agree with you. But if it's at all possible... Well, let's not make it any messier than we have to."

"We can only react to the situation as it unfolds," DJ said from the back, his head down, and his body rocking back and forth. "The plan is always the first casualty after contact with the enemy." He sighed. "I ain't makin' no promises, Savvy, but quarter will be given. Until one of 'em pulls a gun or knife. Then, it's Katy bar the door."

"Roger that," Savannah said. "That's all I ask. Be careful."

"We go in with phones at full volume," Charity ordered. "Loud and disruptive, with overwhelming force. We neutralize the two in front, then DJ and Paul move to the third person in the back room, clearing any other rooms as you go. Doesn't matter if they hear instructions from our phones at this point. This whole thing will be over in less than sixty seconds. They won't have time to react. At most there are three people inside and it's likely the two right by the entry will be the only tangos."

"Poppy," Kevin said, "move over here and flip that seat up." He patted the car seat in front of me. "Then you lead the way and get flat against the wall. I'll follow you and do the same. If anything happens, we can cover DJ as he runs for the door with Paul behind him."

"Good plan," DJ said, palming Charity's ultra-slim handgun in his big fist. "Enrique, you stay with the van, *amigo*. Be ready when we come out with Harper."

I folded the back of my seat down, then flipped the whole thing forward into the footwell, allowing maximum exit room on that side.

"Okay, Enrique," Charity said, taking a deep breath. "Pull up to the driveway and stop right behind the van."

Enrique started the engine, but left the headlights turned off. The moon was more than bright enough.

As he pulled to the curb in front of the house and stopped, Savannah's voice came over their phones. "All clear on the street. No movement inside. Go! Go!"

Instantly, I slid the door back as Charity threw open the front passenger door and charged around the hood of the van with her bullpup rifle. She stopped and covered the street for a moment as Kevin and I moved quickly up the sidewalk, then she fell in behind Paul, as they all ran up the steps and onto the porch.

I moved to the left side of the door, back against the wall, carbine ready, as Kevin moved into a similar position on the opposite side. We exchanged a quick nod of support.

DJ didn't slow at all. Taking the first step with his prosthetic, then planting his good foot on the porch, and launching his prosthetic foot at a spot above the doorknob, he kicked downward with the force of a bull. Wood splintered and the door gave way, crashing into an interior wall.

DJ followed the door, rolling forward, and coming up in a shooting stance, covering to the right of the entry.

Paul was right behind DJ, aiming over DJ's head.

Charity breezed through the door, Kevin right beside her.

I scanned. Still no movement outside.

The DB9 in DJ's hand boomed.

Paul turned and fired also, as Charity brought her rifle to bear on two men with guns, one in a chair and the other on a couch, both with blood already soaking the fronts of their shirts.

Suddenly, one of the dead men moved. Snake and crocodile tattooed arms reached from behind, a sawed off shotgun swinging toward DJ.

Charity fired and the crack of her rifle was joined by three more shots.

The tattooed man's body was slammed against the far wall from the impact of four bullets to his chest.

Apparently the two men on the couch had looked like a single heat signature to Chyrel.

"Three armed tangos down," Charity said.

I swung back around. Still quiet on the street.

A high-pitched scream came from the back of the house, and DJ moved quickly down the hall in that direction, Paul right behind him.

With Kevin covering, Charity checked the three men.

They were all dead.

Suddenly, Paul reappeared. "DJ's got Harper! Let's get the hell out of here!"

Enrique mashed the accelerator to the floor then turned on the headlights as we headed north into Campeche, the narrow streets swallowing us quickly.

"Take it easy," Charity cautioned him, looking back through the van's rear window. "We're good, nobody's following us."

Enrique slowed, and I looked down at Harper, on the floor between DJ and Paul in the middle row. I couldn't believe it. We found her. We actually found her. And she was alive.

A flood of memories of finding Doug alive after he'd

been kidnapped hit my exhausted brain. He'd been alive. Only to betray me. And Chris.

"Are you okay, Harper?" Charity asked.

"Who… who are you?" she managed to get out. Then recognition dawned on her. She sat upright, and shrank back. "But you're Savannah's friend. What's going on?"

DJ turned away from the window and smiled at the girl. "It's okay. We're all friends of Savannah."

"Are you hurt?" Charity asked, taking a bottle of water from Enrique's cooler between the seats, and handing it to her.

With a mixed expression of relief and confusion, Harper tried to take the bottle, struggling with her hands still tied.

"Here, let me help you with that," Paul said, taking a locking knife from a pouch on his belt and clicking it open. He quickly parted the ropes that bound her.

"Friends of Savannah?" Realization that she'd been rescued started to set in. She accepted the bottle and turned it up to her mouth.

"They are," Kevin said from the back. "Poppy and I only just met her today." He took his phone from his pocket and handed it to the girl. "Here. She's on the line now and your mom is right there with her."

Harper grabbed the phone and put it to her ear as she burst into sobs. "Mom?"

Her voice echoed in the van, coming from everyone else's phones, startling her.

"Savannah?" Harper asked, nervously. "Is anyone there?" She looked up at Kevin as if he'd played a dirty trick. "There's nobody there."

Then her eyes locked onto me. "You have red hair. Red hair." She turned inward, as though trying to sort something out. "It must have been red hair."

"What are you talking about?" Charity asked. "Does that mean something?"

She shook her head, obviously exhausted. "I thought they were talking about a red horse. "

No way. Couldn't be.

"A red horse?" Charity asked, as Enrique turned and headed toward the pier.

"I overheard them talking," Harper replied, then turned back to me. "They thought I didn't know any Spanish, so I was able to pick up a few things."

I nodded, trying to encourage her, afraid if I spoke she'd clam up.

"Someone called and told the tattooed guy something that made him angry. He got another call just a few minutes later and he nearly flipped out. They put me in the van and drove around all morning." She paused as though sorting through the timeline was too confusing. "I thought they said they were looking for a red horse and were going to kill it, but"—she looked back to Charity—"horse and hair sound a lot alike in Spanish."

Charity nodded, "Cabello rojo and caballo rojo, easy mistake."

An innocent conservation intern at the turtle camp had made the same translation error when the cartel had kidnapped her instead of me. They'd been looking for me specifically. Because Doug had sent them after me. But I had been on the west coast when all that went down. They couldn't possibly be…

"We drove around most of the morning. Finally, they opened the door of the van and made me sit in front of it while the tattooed guy took a picture." Her eyes swung back around to me. "They must have been looking for you. El cabello rojo."

"The proof of life photo," Charity said with a sigh, then looked up at me. "It was you. They were killing two birds with one stone. Proof of life and a direct threat toward you. They must've been alerted by corrupt authorities when you entered the country. The cartel put a bounty on your head"

Shit. Dalton was right. Back then, I had busted the cartel boss.

"I don't understand," said Harper, staring at me. "Were they after you instead of me?"

Charity continued, matter-of-fact, one colleague to another. "I don't think you're safe in Mexico."

"She's right!" Harper exclaimed, her eyes darting from me to Charity and back. "After they took the picture, they blindfolded me again and took me to a smelly old shack and the tattooed man called someone and told him to find and kill the red horse. Someone's going to try to kill you!"

"It's okay," DJ said in a soothing tone, placing his hand softly on her shoulder. "He already tried and my partner, Charity, stopped the guy. It doesn't matter. You're safe now. We're all safe."

"What happened after the tattooed man made the call?" Paul asked, his voice calm as always.

His voice was doing double the work because the reality was starting to dawn on me too. There was a hit out for me. And I'd walked right into town.

I drew in a breath, then slowly exhaled.

Harper was shaking. "Then we took off again, and they drove to that place you found me. They started drinking and laughing about the red horse. I was locked in a room, but—" She started to hyperventilate. "I could hear them snoring for at least an hour before you got there and..."

"Got you out safely," I said, enunciating each word. This girl had been through too much. I leaned forward and stroked her hair. "That's all you need to concentrate on, okay. You're safe now. Don't worry about me."

"That's right," Paul agreed. "You've been through a terrible ordeal and you're safe now. That's all you need to concern yourself with tonight. In just a few minutes, you'll be back with your mom and shortly after that, home and safe."

"Is Harper all right?" Savannah's urgent voice came from every phone,

"Yes!" Harper shouted. "I'm okay! Thank you, Savannah! Whatever you did, thank you! Is my mom with you?"

Charity took her phone out and disconnected from the call, nodding at the others to do the same, so Harper and her mother could talk privately.

"What happened to you, Savvy," DJ asked, before he disconnected. "You disappeared from the com again."

"As soon as Charity said the cartel men were down, I went to get Suzette. Here she is now, Harper."

"Baby?" Suzette's voice came over Kevin's speaker, as DJ disconnected.

"Mom!" she squealed.

Kevin took his phone from Harper, turned the speaker off, then returned it to her.

She put the phone to her ear. "I'm here mom! I can see the pier ahead!" Then the sobbing came.

Tears welled in my eyes for her. She was safe now–her ordeal finally over.

I glanced over at Enrique, who had a tear running down his cheek. He smiled. "*Viva la gente libre.*"

"Long live the free people," Charity agreed. Then she looked ahead toward the long pier. "The head's been cut off the snake, Enrique," she said softly. "And the crocodile, too, I suppose. It will be up to you and the people of Campeche to keep the serpent from growing another."

Enrique parked and everyone piled out of the van, all weapons carefully concealed inside Charity's camera case.

I reminded him about the bag of turtles, and he assured me he'd take them to the conservation center right away.

The customs guard at the gate barely paid any attention to the group of gringo cruisers, and we quickly climbed down to the waiting tender.

As we motored out, with Paul at the helm, Charity sat next to Harper on the small bench, forward of the helm. Ahead of them, Kevin stood in the bow, scanning for any boat traffic.

DJ stood in the stern watching for any possible threat behind us. I sat next to him, comfortable that this group had us covered for the moment, aware the threat wasn't over. I had to get out of Mexico as soon as possible. My presence put all of them in danger. I searched the airlines for our quickest way out.

A text pinged on my phone. It was Chris: Is tonight going to work or what?

What irony. I just might make it back in time. I scanned the flights. Nothing worked.

"The earliest I can get us on is a ten o'clock to DFW," I said to Kevin. "Back to New Orleans by tomorrow night." Another day I'd have to put Chris off.

DJ looked up, grinning. "Nawlins? How ya tryin' to get there?"

"Commercial," I replied, then looked back at Kevin. "That's the best I can find."

DJ looked over at Charity. "I think they've been a great asset," he said. "And us working with other agencies is always a good thing. Ain't that what Mr. Armstrong always says? Nawlins ain't much out of our way."

"You have a plane?" I asked, not surprised.

Charity nodded at DJ.

"Not just any old plane," DJ said, checking his watch. "In fact, if you two agree to buy the first round, I think we can get ya to Lafitte's Blacksmith Bar before last call."

The memory of being puked on by that drunk tourist made my stomach flip.

"I thought you were going back to Florida," Charity said.

"Not if our new friends need a lift," DJ replied. "That'd just be rude." Then his eyes sparkled. "Hey, we should all go. The G-550 can get us there by three, easy. And Nawlins never sleeps."

"I have to meet with Savannah in the morning," Charity said, to DJ's obvious disappointment. "We have to… uh… debrief and all that."

"Think she'd mind if the plane goes to Nawlins, on its way to Fort Meade, instead of stopping in Florida?"

"How will you get home?"

Kevin leaned closer, as Paul turned the boat toward *MollySue's* stern. "I'm sure WCEA will cover that in exchange for a ride for the two of us."

"It's settled then," DJ said to Charity. "We're all buggin' out, except for you and Savvy?"

She smiled at him and nodded.

When the tender pulled up to *MollySue's* swim platform, Suzette and Jojo were there waiting.

"Harper!" she called.

The girl climbed over the side of the boat and fell into her mother's arms. I turned to hide the tears that formed in my eyes.

"Grab your gear, Jojo," DJ said. "Our plane leaves in thirty minutes."

"Suzette, you should have the captain leave here as soon as possible," Charity said. "We have a plane on standby, arriving in New Orleans tonight. Grab what you and Harper need and you'll be in your own bed before the sun comes up."

Chapter Twenty-Four

"I need two minutes," I said to Kevin. "I'll be right there."

The plane was readying for our flight back to the states. But I had something I needed to do that couldn't wait.

I called Dalton.

He answered right away. "Hello, Poppy? Everything okay?"

"Yes. We found her. Alive. And I love you. I love you."

Silence.

"Are you there?"

"Yes. I love you, too. What happened? Are you all right?"

"Yeah. I'll tell you all about it when I get back. Boarding a plane now. But I just couldn't wait to tell you."

"That you love me?"

"Yes, that I love you."

"I'm glad."

"And you were right."

"I was. About what?"

"About everything."

"Wow, I'm... speechless. Wait, is this Poppy? Poppy McVie?"

"I gotta go."

"I'll meet you at the airport."

The thought of seeing Earl right now made me sigh. "I know I just told you I love you, but I'm so exhausted. I just can't..."

Dalton read my mind. "Hyland cut him loose."

"What?" My vision blurred. "You can't be serious?"

"Apparently, the moment you got Harper, the judge revealed the blackmailer. It wasn't Earl."

"So she just let him go? But she hasn't even talked to me. We were right. One of the bunchers came to the encampment where they had her. It's all connected." *Dammit!*

"Poppy, you know how it is. We've had this—"

"But she never listens to us, the ones on the ground. We're the ones out here, in the trenches, and—"

"I know, but we have to—"

Dammit! "It's always the same crap."

"Yes, it is."

"I'll see you in a few hours."

I sat next to Kevin in the plane, a G-550 with plush, cream-colored leather seating and exceptionally large, oval windows. Armstrong was definitely well-funded, not working on a government budget. *Must be nice.*

I bet Armstrong actually listens to his people.

As soon as we were in the air, I eased the seat back and a leg rest popped up. "I could get used to this," I said.

Kevin grinned. "You'd like to work for Armstrong?"

"What?" With Charity and DJ? "No. Not my style."

"Well, what about WCEA? We could really use a talent like you. And you and I make a great team."

I sat back upright. "Are you serious?"

"Yes, of course I'm serious. You're an impressive agent. I meant every word I said. You had me with your Brittany act, hook, line, and sinker. And then here in Mexico. You never hesitated, not for a moment."

I felt the familiar pink flush to my face. "I didn't do anything anyone else wouldn't have done."

"Maybe. But I know you looked at our suspect list for about two minutes, and when you saw that guy, you knew him right away. And remembered his name. How'd you do that?"

I shrugged. I just did.

"That's amazing. You're amazing. I'm calling my boss the minute we land. Name your salary."

I stared. My salary?

"Believe me. We're well funded. Maybe not Armstrong-level funding, but name your price. I'll make it happen."

I stared some more. Was he serious? Name my salary? Any amount I wanted?

Is that what I wanted? To leave my government job and go after wildlife traffickers with Kevin. No more Hyland. No tied hands all the time. Working with someone who actually respects me, my thoughts.

I leaned back in the soft recliner and looked around the posh plane. I was exhausted. Was this even real?

Harper was snuggled in her mom's arms, sound asleep. Her mother's eyes were red, but she was wide awake, staring at me, a smile on her face. Maybe Earl had been cut loose, but Harper was alive and in her mother's arms. That's what mattered.

I'd helped make that happen. That was real.

I glanced back at Kevin. He was staring at me. "Whatever you're thinking, I'll double it."

My eyebrows shot up. Was this guy for real? I'd never really thought about the money before. I'd been stuffing my paycheck into an account I'd opened when I started work as an intern. Most of it went to rent on my crappy one room apartment I hadn't been to in months.

If I listened to my mother, I should be planning, budgeting, saving more for retirement. It would happen, some day, I supposed. Like Joe. I pictured him sitting in the diner across from me. How restless he had been. What had he called it, unbearable? Everything's in slow motion, he'd said. Didn't sound like something to look forward to.

Right now, I had what I'd always wanted. The Presidential Animal Task Force was the pinnacle of a career. And I'd achieved that already. But, if I were honest, it wasn't at all what I'd thought it was going to be. Right now it felt like a whole lot more hassle with the same old results. Jerks like Earl got to keep on being jerks, hurting animals. What was it all for?

Every case I'd worked on added up to a tiny drop in the bucket. If that. I should've listened to my dad. He had always said, cut off one ugly head and two grow in its place. That's probably all that happened when he died, trying to… trying to what?

To know what happened to my dad. I couldn't think of anything I wanted more.

I sat back upright. "Does your organization have any cases currently in Africa?"

"Africa? You want to go to Africa? Sure, we can make that happen. Where do you want to go?"

This guy was nuts. "Just name a place? You can't be serious."

"You're going to love working for us." He leaned

forward. "The best part is, no badge." And he gave me a wink.

No badge. And no Dalton. Even if Kevin also offered him a job, too, there was no way he would agree. It just wasn't in his DNA. He would stay the course. Slow and steady. Always… always have my back.

I turned to gaze out the window.

I had just told Dalton I loved him.

Dalton. My career. Africa. Could I have it all? My heart wanted to believe I could. But my head knew I'd have to choose.

"You don't have to say yes right now. But remember, the sky's the limit with us," Kevin said. "Just think on it."

Think on it. A job with no badge. Anywhere I wanted to go. Getting paid any amount I wanted to be paid.

I laid my head back and stared at the exit sign until the grumble of the landing gear brought me back to Earth.

After Kevin and I said our goodbyes to DJ and the others, declining their offer for drinks at Lafitte's, we walked down the stairs into the thick night air and crossed the tarmac.

Dalton was there, leaning on the fence, in those tight jeans and that leisurely cowboy stance. For a moment, I couldn't believe he was my boyfriend. Had I just told him I loved him? A little shiver came over me. Oh my god, I had. I wanted to run to him, throw my arms around him. But I held back. He wouldn't want to make our relationship known. We'd keep it professional. As always.

"Hey, welcome back," he said as he pushed himself from the fence. "How was the flight? Did you get some shuteye?"

"Not exactly. But we did find Harper. That's what matters."

"I want to hear all about it. We've got a table waiting for us at a little wine spot we thought you'd like."

"We?"

"Yeah, me and Chris."

"You talked to Chris?"

"Yeah, of course."

I stared. *Of course?*

"He's there holding a table. We've gotta get going. Kevin, I assume you'll join us."

Kevin nodded. "Wouldn't miss it. I've been wanting to talk to you for a long time."

"Yeah, I figured. I've got a few questions for you, too."

We all laughed.

On the way to the bar, Kevin and I told him the highlights of our search for Harper. Kevin didn't give details about how close I'd come to being shot in the back of the head, which I appreciated. I'd have to find a way to tell Dalton about that later.

Or maybe I wouldn't.

In what seemed like minutes, we arrived at Bacchanal Wine Shop, a charming, rustic old building that looked like it had been plucked from a tiny village in Italy and plopped down on this out-of-the-way street just outside the French Quarter. Strings of lights stretched among the live oaks, the bulbs glowing a warm amber over a yard alive with people chatting while a band played a bluesy Cajun ballad.

Kevin excused himself to find the restroom.

I spotted Chris at a large table, but he wasn't alone. He was happily chatting with someone—a good-looking someone. I grabbed Dalton by the elbow.

"Wait. Who is that he's with?"

"I don't know. He didn't mention anyone."

"Maybe he met him here. He looks like he's really

enjoying himself. Maybe we should give them some time, you know."

Dalton took my hand. "C'mon. He's been worried about you. And if that guy is boyfriend potential, he'll have to explain you sooner or later."

"What's that supposed to mean?"

Dalton grinned. "You know I missed you. Terribly."

"Terribly?"

"Excruciatingly."

"Is that a word?"

"It's a feeling, for sure."

My cheeks turned a little pink. "I know. I just like hearing you say it. We're not going to be here long, right?"

His eyes got that look. "As long as we can stand it."

Just then Chris turned and saw me, and I couldn't hold back. I ran across the yard, weaving through the array of tables and chairs, and launched into his arms. "I'm so glad you came."

"Whoa, Poppy girl, what has gotten into you?"

"Nothing. Really. It's just been a crazy couple of days." I looked at the other guy who was now on his feet. "And who is this?"

"Chad, Poppy. Chad and I just met. You don't mind if he joins us do you?"

"Are you kidding? We'd love it." I gave him a wink. "As long as I get to pick the wine."

"Why, of course, my dear." It was his turn to wink at Chad. "Poppy's a total wine snob."

"The term is sommelier."

"That's what I said."

Kevin appeared and he and Dalton made their introductions while I scanned the wine list.

Chris slipped his arm in mine. "We have to order at the bar. We'll be right back," he said, and tugged me after him.

We weren't five steps away before Chris started in. "You need to stop with the thing with Dalton and Africa."

I spun on him. "What? How do you—? Dalton told you to say that?"

He looked offended. "Seriously? I know how you are."

"Like a dog with a bone," we said simultaneously.

He tugged me along. "And you're just going to damage this relationship."

"Me? He's the one who went, without telling me, got information he's still not telling me, like he's trying to protect me or something."

We got to the bar. There was a short line.

"And what's wrong with that?"

"What's wrong with that? I'm not a child, and that's not how adult relationships work."

"You are something," he said, shaking his head.

I couldn't believe it. "Not you, too?"

"Has it occurred to you that maybe *you* should trust *him*?"

I stared.

"And maybe he's not holding back anything from you."

I shook my head. "No. I know Dalton. He knows way more than he's telling me."

"Okay, maybe that's true. But maybe, and just maybe, that's because he knows he doesn't have the entire story, and there's no point in giving you a bunch of bits that don't add up. Maybe he never will have the whole story. Maybe you never will."

"But he doesn't get to decide that for me. This isn't just about me knowing about my dad. It's about trust."

"Are you sure?"

"Chris, what is it with you?"

The young lady behind the bar spoke up. "Got an order?"

I hadn't realized we'd shuffled forward. Chris had his credit card out. I quickly told her what we wanted and turned back to him.

"I don't understand any of this. Dalton didn't trust me to go to Mexico."

"Did he stop you?"

"Well, no. But he was worried."

"Of course he was. Poppy girl, there's a big difference between trusting someone and being worried. He loves you. He gets to be worried." He smirked. "And believe me, he was. He was pacing around like a cat in a cage."

I didn't know what to say. "I can't believe you two talked. I didn't know you were even in touch."

Chris shrugged. "See, there's a lot you don't know. Not all of it's bad."

"Okay. I get your point. I'll talk to Dalton."

He put his arm around my waist and pulled me toward him as we walked back toward the guys. "I was worried, too."

"You know I have a dangerous job, but I'm well trained and can handle myself."

"Yeah, that's not what I've been worried about. You haven't been yourself lately."

"Yeah, well, living with Earl hasn't exactly been a walk in the park."

"It's not Earl."

I stopped and turned to face him. "What is it? You haven't been yourself either. I've been worried about you."

"Me? I'm just depressed, you know, normal for what I've been through, but I'm doing better. But it doesn't help to be worried about you, too."

"I'm fine."

He put his hands on my shoulders. "You're not fine. Here we are talking about trust. And what I'm seeing is that you've…" He hesitated. "You seemed to have lost trust in yourself."

Had I? Isn't that what Joe had been trying to tell me? To trust my gut. Trust myself. Chris was right. I was struggling with that lately. But why? What had happened to me?

Chris took my hand. "C'mon. We can talk some more later."

Dalton stood up as we approached and offered me a chair, and we all settled into our seats and the casual conversation of people who barely know each other.

Without giving up too much, Kevin kindly explained to Chad how we'd all come to meet and end up working on a case together.

"So people sell turtles for a living? And it's illegal?" he asked, genuinely intrigued.

"Depends on the species, but yes," Kevin said. "From Louisiana alone, more than sixteen million wild-caught turtles were exported in the past five years. Mostly to China. And that's only the numbers that have been tracked, which don't include illegal totals. Though there are claims that most are not actually wild-caught, as labelled, but are hatchlings that were, and are, produced from existing breeding stock on licensed turtle farms. But that raises another issue about how those farms are stocked."

The weight of the last few days caught up to me all at once. I wasn't sure how long I'd last before nodding off.

Chad seemed genuinely interested so Kevin plowed on. "Most states have put restrictions in place to halt the decline of turtles, but the state of Louisiana has, so far, failed to do so, declining petitions from conservation organizations. It's the only state that allows unrestricted harvesting and trade of most of its turtle species. The legal turtle farms actually make the situation worse. This region is a hotbed of illegal activity."

Chris joined in. "Turtle crime? Who knew?"

Kevin continued, "Turtles in particular can be very lucrative because they are notoriously easy to smuggle. They make no noise and hardly move. The traffickers will duct tape their legs to their shells and shove them inside anything they'll fit into—cereal boxes, suitcases, even Pringles cans. Sometimes they stuff them down their pants."

I tried to hide a yawn. I was exhausted, but my mind was whirring over Chris's words. Why wasn't I trusting myself? Maybe he was right about Dalton. I had the urge to slip my hand in his.

Kevin kept on. "Last year, a moron got caught trying to smuggle a turtle onto a plane disguised as a hamburger. The poor animal was smooshed between a couple of buns, a slice of tomato, and some lettuce."

Chad stared, open-mouthed.

"Take for example the guy we've been after. He's been shoving them in overnight express boxes and shipping them through the U.S. mail to China. Even if we—"

My whole body snapped to attention. "What?" I gaped.

Kevin swung around to face me. "Huh?"

"What did you just say? The post office? He's been shipping using the post office?"

"Yeah, I told you—"

My heart zoomed to beating double-time. "No, you didn't. You never mentioned it."

"I'm sure I did, when you—"

I turned to Dalton. "It's Earl. He's the exporter. Right under our noses. Unbelievable!" I shot up from the chair. "We gotta go!"

"Wait. What?" Kevin was saying as he slowly rose to his feet.

"Sandy, his girlfriend. She works for the post office. She said something"—I turned back to Dalton, who was also on his feet—"the night at the dance, about him using her for her job. I thought—"

"—she meant for the benefits," he finished my sentence. "Big package. I'm gonna kill him."

"And she was there, that day at the park. I totally forgot to ask about that because we'd seen you. And then... you know." Ugh, that embarrassment. "Why was she there? She had to be the one sending the texts and emails."

"Makes sense, I guess," Kevin said, trying to catch up.

A young lady appeared with a bottle of wine and five glasses.

I gave Chris a kiss on the cheek. "Enjoy the tempranillo. We've gotta go!"

Dalton was already at a dead run for the car. Kevin and I sprinted to catch up to him.

At the dock, we ditched the truck and got into the airboat. Dalton didn't say a word as he fired it up, grabbed hold of the stick, and slammed the pedal down.

The swamp at night is a dense wall of black. I couldn't see a thing, but he seemed hellbent on getting there fast, blasting around corners, putting the boat up on edge.

As we swung around the last bend, Dalton finally let up. I could barely make out the houseboat, anchored right where it had been all along. No lights were on, but Earl's fishing boat was tied off to the side.

Dalton rammed the airboat into the side of the houseboat and leapt off the side onto the deck.

"Earl, you son-of-a-bitch, get your sorry ass outta bed!"

he called as he disappeared inside while Kevin and I scrambled to get lines tied off.

The bedroom light flicked on as I heard a loud splash from the back side of the houseboat. Earl must've gone out the window.

I turned on the living room light. Kevin stood beside me.

"The gators'll get him," he said with a grin.

Then a second splash. I ran to the bedroom window. Dalton had gone in after him.

"What the hell?" Kevin said, heading toward the window.

"There's a spotlight." I ran to the kitchen cabinets, tossed a broom, dustpan, garbage can out of the way. It was here somewhere. On the shelf.

I grabbed it and clicked it on, blinding Kevin.

"Sorry!" I pushed past him, back to the bedroom window and shined it in the water. Earl was thrashing around. Something tugged at him from below.

Kevin leaned over me. "Does he know what he's doing?"

I grinned. "He was a SEAL."

"Really? A Navy SEAL?"

I laughed. "Is there any other kind?"

Kevin shook his head. "Yeah, but the gators."

I pushed the thought aside.

Earl's head popped up and he gasped for air, then he was pulled down again.

Kevin let out a puff of air. "That poor bastard doesn't stand a chance."

I grinned again.

Chapter Twenty-Five

Earl sat at the table with his defense attorney, slumped forward, his back to us. It seemed Dalton had knocked the cocky right out of him.

Hyland had arrived at the last minute, strolling into the court room and sitting down right next to me, saying nothing. As the court reporter got seated and other officials shuffled about, she leaned my way. "The judge claimed the blackmail pertained to another case."

Was she explaining herself? Justifying letting Earl off?

"A Marcus Thompson. Drug related."

"Are we sure there's no tie to Earl? I mean, it's possible the cartel would—"

"I know, McVie. It's possible. I read your report. I've contacted the DEA and alerted them to the likely connection."

I stared. Really?

"We've got other priorities."

The side door opened and we were told to rise. Judge Landry came through, straight to the bench. He was younger than I'd expected. He had just a hint of gray hair around the edge of his temple. Probably tinged from the forty-eight hours his daughter had been held by the cartel.

I admired his calm and professionalism. If it were me, I'd leap over the bench and wring Earl's neck with my bare hands. But that was the difference between me and him—he had the power of that gavel.

The charges against Earl were read, including defrauding the government because we'd provided a list of witnesses who claimed he'd been buying turtles from locals while using the bookmobile airboat.

"I understand you have something to add," the judge stated, looking at me.

"Yes, your honor," I said, rising to my feet. "During our undercover investigation, Sandy Davidson, the defendant's girlfriend and co-conspirator, revealed that the defendant had shot and killed a protected species on March twenty-second. I've confirmed that indeed, a whooping crane, a CITES Appendix one species, had been killed on that date near the described location, and I have requested ballistics. We suspect they will confirm that the defendant indeed was the shooter. I ask that this atrocity be added to the long list of crimes of depraved indifference with which he has been accused."

"So added," the judge said with what I was sure was a nod.

He shuffled some papers then said, "The defendant is remanded to the parish jail until trial. This court is adjourned." He slammed down the gavel with a satisfying thud.

Earl slowly turned to face me and I saw it in his eyes: begrudging respect. I gave him a wink.

I turned to leave, satisfied that, as far as Earl was concerned, Judge Landry would take it from here, and saw Joe sitting a few rows back.

"You needed another excuse to get out of that retirement village, did you?" I said, heading for him.

"Any reason will do," he said, pulling me into a bear hug. "I wanted to tell you in person how proud I am of you."

My cheeks flushed with embarrassment. "Thank you. You truly have no idea how much that means to me."

"So, what's next?"

"We wait for ballistics, some data from the phone company. You know, the usual."

He tilted his head forward. "I meant for you."

I shrugged.

He waited a long moment before he said, "I happened to run into Kevin over there." He gestured in Kevin's direction. "He mentioned he's offered you a job. Asked me my thoughts. Honestly, I wasn't sure what you'd want me to say."

"Well..." I stared at my hero, my mentor, my friend. "What *are* your thoughts?"

"Oh no." He shook his head. "Doesn't work that way, my dear. This is your decision. Only you can decide. My job is to support you, no matter what you choose."

I looked to the back of the courtroom where Dalton and Kevin stood chatting. Then turned back to Joe. "I'm not sure."

He nodded. "I remember feeling that way a lot when I was young. Now I'm sure of even less."

That made me smile.

"But I do know, that if I had to do it all over again, I wouldn't change a thing. Sure, I had my fair share of frustrating ops. Some I ended up getting another stab at. Some never went my way. But as I look back now, I can say I did something. I made a difference. What more can one man want?"

"A difference?" I said. "You're a legend. A hero. A superhero."

He placed his hand on my shoulder. "So are you, my dear. So are you." He hugged me, then said, "I must take my leave. You wear the cape now and you have to decide what to do with it."

I watched him walk away, trying to process what he'd just said, when Sara popped into my view.

I didn't realize she'd come.

"So, maybe you'll be able to prove he shot our bird after all," she said as she offered her hand. "I'm glad. But I have to ask, with all the other counts against him, why bother with that one. It's a slap on the wrist compared to the rest."

"Maybe," I said, trying to get my head back. "But every little conviction helps. Maybe the next time, some idiot thinks twice before pulling the trigger. Maybe a little line in the news will create a little more awareness. Maybe it's simply about doing what's right because justice matters."

She cocked her head to the side.

"Okay, maybe because I swore I'd nail him for it."

She smiled wide. "I see." She paused as though pondering something. "And the other issue you were dealing with. Any new insight on that?"

I thought for a moment. "Maybe. Yes, I think so. But…"

She waited, politely giving me space.

"I'm just not sure. You know, with these kinds of decisions, I want to be sure."

"Oh honey." She put her hand on mine and squeezed. "Life doesn't work that way. We almost never get a chance to be one-hundred percent sure. Sometimes you've got to decide, and all you're sure of, is fifty-one percent. Or eighty-two percent. Either way, you have to move forward."

I looked to the back of the courtroom where Dalton and Kevin waited.

She squeezed my hand a little harder. "But I have a feeling it's not that."

"Really?" I looked back to her.

"I think you know exactly what you want, but something else is clouding that decision."

Until that moment, I hadn't known what that was. But now I knew.

Author's Note

I hope you enjoyed this story. Thank YOU so much for reading. If you're interested in connecting with me online, I like to share travel stories (like my own trip to Louisiana) and videos, my wildlife photos, and MORE! Follow me at www.KimberliBindschatel.com. You'll be the FIRST to know about my new releases, too. Join the adventure.

What will Poppy do next?

Can't get enough of Poppy McVie? Courageous, smart, adventurous, caring and tough as nails, Poppy is on to her next page-turning mission fighting wildlife crimes in her own, no-holds-barred style while sparks continue to fly with sexy Dalton.

The next book in the series is in the works.

Check here to sign up to be notified with details.

The Poppy McVie Adventure Mystery Series

Operation Tropical Affair

Operation Orca Rescue

Operation Grizzly Camp

Operation Turtle Ransom

Operation Arctic Deception

Operation Dolphin Spirit

Operation Wolf Pack

Operation Bayou Justice

Thanks

Thanks to John Smart for letting me pick your legal brain over jambalaya. Thank you Sonny Fontenot for the wealth of local knowledge as well as the history of turtle issues in Louisiana. And Oliver Ljustina, your info gave me some great ideas. Thank you.

Rachel, as usual, you helped me sort out where Poppy was struggling. You're the best!

Thank you Alexa for jumping in at the last minute. Your insight was invaluable.

I get to do this because of the loving support of my husband.

As always, thanks to my parents for raising me with a deep love of animals.

Most of all, thank YOU for reading and supporting this author.

About the Author

Born and raised in Michigan, I spent summers at the lake, swimming, catching frogs, and chasing fireflies, winters building things out of cardboard and construction paper, writing stories, and dreaming of faraway places. Since I didn't make honors English in high school, I thought I couldn't write. So I started hanging out in the art room. The day I borrowed a camera, my love affair with photography began. Long before the birth of the pixel, I was exposing real silver halides to light and marveling at the magic of an image appearing on paper under a red light.

After college, I freelanced in commercial photography studios. During the long days of rigging strobes, stories skipped through my mind. As happens in life though, I was possessed by another dream—to be a wildlife photographer. I trekked through the woods to find loons, grizzly bears, whales, and moose. Then, for six years, I put my heart and soul into publishing a nature magazine, *Whisper in the Woods*. But it was not meant to be my magnum opus. This time, my attention was drawn skyward. I'd always been fascinated by the aurora borealis, shimmering in the night sky, but now my focus went beyond, to the cosmos, to wonder about our place in the universe.

In the spring of 2010, I sat down at the computer, started typing words, and breathed life into a curious boy named Kiran in *The Path to the Sun*. Together, in our quest for truth, Kiran and I have explored the mind and spirit. Our journey has taken us to places of new perspective. Alas, the answers always seem just beyond our grasp, as elusive as a firefly on a warm autumn night.

Most recently, my focus has shifted to more pressing issues—imperiled wildlife. With the Poppy McVie series, I hope to bring some light into the shadowy underworld of black market wildlife trade, where millions of wild animals are captured or slaughtered annually to fund organized crime. IT. MUST. STOP.

If you'd like to learn more and stay in touch, please follow me at www.KimberliBindschatel.com

www.ingramcontent.com/pod-product-compliance
Lightning Source LLC
Chambersburg PA
CBHW032209300425
25955CB00032B/354

* 9 7 8 1 6 4 8 3 9 7 8 9 9 *